Happy 1st Birthday Keaton!
We Love you
Aunt Tracie
Uncle Steb

My First Treasury

Parragon

Bath • New York • Cologne • Melbourne • Delhi
Hong Kong • Shenzhen • Singapore • Amsterdam

This edition published by Parragon Books Ltd in 2014 and distributed by

Parragon Inc.
440 Park Avenue South, 13th Floor
New York, NY 10016
www.parragon.com

ISBN 978-1-4723-1137-5

Printed in China

Contents

Hey Diddle Diddle 9

Here We Go Round the Mulberry Bush 10

Five Little Monkeys 12

Pat-a-Cake 14

The Grand Old Duke of York 15

Humpty Dumpty 16

Baa, Baa, Black Sheep 17

Little Jack Horner 18

Ring Around the Rosie 19

The Three Billy Goats Gruff 20

One, Two, Three, Four, Five 26

Itsy Bitsy Spider 27

Polly, Put the Kettle On 28

The Gingerbread Man 29

The Queen of Hearts 36

There Was an Old Woman 38

Mary, Mary, Quite Contrary 39

Bobby Shaftoe 40

This Little Piggy 41

The Naughty Bears 42

Ten Little Teddy Bears 48

Lazy Mary 50

Lucy Locket 52

Nippy Snippy 53

Whale Song 54

My Best Friend 60

Some Teddy Bears 61

Ding Dong Bell 62

Lazy Teddy 63
If You're Happy and You Know It 68
Elephants Never Forget 69
Itchy Spots 70
Teddy Bears' Picnic 71
Little Dog Lost 72
Round and Round the Garden 78
The Bear Will Have to Go 79
In a Spin 84
There Was a Crooked Man 85
Knick Knack Paddy Whack 86
The Littlest Pig 88
Achoo! 93
Giddyup, Teddy &
Three Bears in a Tub 94
Midnight Fun 95
Birthday Bunnies 96
Jack Be Nimble 103
Happy Hippopotamus 104

Boys and Girls, Come Out to Play 106

Tea with the Queen 108

Barney the Boastful Bear 110

Pop Goes the Weasel &
Two Little Men in a Flying Saucer 117

There Was an Old Woman Tossed Up
in a Blanket 118

The Ugly Duckling 120

Claude, the Lonely Crocodile 128

Old MacDonald Had a Farm 135

The Princess and the Pea 138

Sleep, Little Child 143

The Wheels on the Bus 144

Thumbelina 146

Sing a Song of
Sixpence 154

Lavender's Blue 155
Mary Had a Little Lamb 156
Three Blind Mice 157
Little Miss Muffet 158
Rub-a-dub-dub 159
Pussycat, Pussycat 160
Row, Row, Row Your Boat 161
The Fast and Flashy Fish 162
Henny-Penny 169
The Wolf and the Raccoon 174
Tom Thumb 180
Ug–Ug–Ugly 188
Star Light, Star Bright 195
It's Raining, It's Pouring 196

Hickory, Dickory, Dock 197
I Had a Little Nut Tree 198
Simple Simon 199
Mrs. Hen 200
Ride a Cock Horse 201
The Frog Prince 202
Runaway Ragtime 209
The Three Little Pigs and the Wolf 216
Polly Penguin Wants to Fly 222
The Naughty Little Rabbits 228
Jungle, Jungle! 234
Roly and Poly 238
Tumbling 245

Brahms's Lullaby 246
We Won't Budge 248
The Man in the Moon 256

Hey Diddle Diddle

Hey diddle diddle,
The cat and the fiddle,
The cow jumped over the moon;
The little dog laughed
To see such sport,
And the dish ran away with the spoon.

Here We Go Round the Mulberry Bush

Here we go round the mulberry bush,
The mulberry bush, the mulberry bush;
Here we go round the mulberry bush,
On a cold and frosty morning.

This is the way we wash our hands,
Wash our hands, wash our hands;
This is the way we wash our hands,
On a cold and frosty morning.

This is the way we brush our hair,
Brush our hair, brush our hair;
This is the way we brush our hair,
On a cold and frosty morning.

This is the way we go to school,
Go to school, go to school;
This is the way we go to school,
On a cold and frosty morning.

Five Little Monkeys

Five little monkeys
walked along the shore;
One went a-sailing,
Then there were four.

Four little monkeys
climbed up a tree;
One of them fell down,
Then there were three.

Three little monkeys
found a pot of glue;
One got stuck in it,
Then there were two.

Two little monkeys
found a raisin bun;
One ran away with it,
Then there was one.

One little monkey
cried all afternoon,
So they put him in an airplane
And sent him to the moon.

Pat-a-Cake

Pat-a-cake, pat-a-cake, baker's man,
Bake me a cake as fast as you can.
Roll it, and prick it, and mark it with a "B"
And put it in the oven for Baby and me!

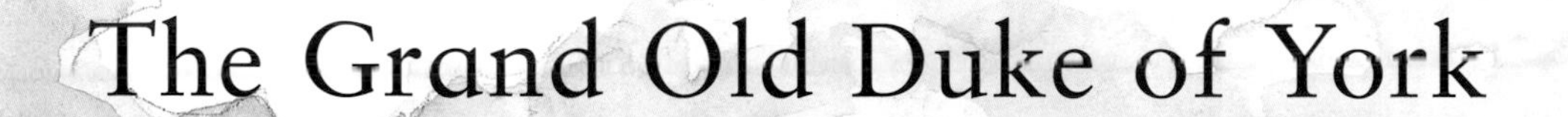

The Grand Old Duke of York

Oh, the grand old Duke of York,
He had ten thousand men,
He marched them up to the top of the hill,
And he marched them down again.

And when they were up they were up,
And when they were down they were down,
And when they were only halfway up,
They were neither up nor down.

Humpty Dumpty

Humpty Dumpty sat on a wall,
Humpty Dumpty had a great fall;
All the king's horses and all the king's men
Couldn't put Humpty together again.

Baa, Baa, Black Sheep

Baa, baa, black sheep,
Have you any wool?
Yes sir, yes sir,
Three bags full;
One for the master,
And one for the dame,
And one for the little boy
Who lives down the lane.

Little Jack Horner

Little Jack Horner
Sat in the corner,
Eating his Christmas pie;
He put in his thumb,
And pulled out a plum,
And said, "What a good boy am I!"

Ring Around the Rosie

Ring around the rosie,
A pocket full of posies.
Ashes! Ashes!
We all fall down!

The Three Billy Goats Gruff

Once, high in some faraway mountains, lived three Billy Goats Gruff. There was a teeny, tiny billy goat, a middle-sized billy goat, and a big, strong billy goat.

One day, when the teeny, tiny Billy Goat Gruff was searching for some juicy grass to eat, he noticed a meadow full of green, green grass on the other side of the river. "Hmm," he thought, "if I could just cross over that bridge and eat some of that grass, I could grow as big as my brothers."

But every smart Billy Goat Gruff knew that an ugly troll lived under the bridge—a troll who was so bad and ugly that any goat who dared to set foot on the bridge was never heard of again.

"I've never seen him," thought the teeny, tiny Billy Goat Gruff. "Perhaps he's moved away. That grass looks so very delicious, I think I'll just tiptoe across and hope for the best!"

So the brave little Billy Goat Gruff tiptoed his way across the bridge.

TRIP, TRAP! TRIP, TRAP! TRIP, TRAP!

went his hooves. He was halfway across the bridge when suddenly... "ROAR!" Out jumped the horrible troll.

"Who's that trip, trapping over my bridge?" roared the troll.

"Only little old me," said the teeny, tiny Billy Goat Gruff. "I'm on my way to the meadow to eat grass. Don't let me disturb you."

"Oh, no, you don't,"

roared the ugly troll. "You've woken me up, and now I'm going to gobble you up."

"But I'm just a skinny thing," said the teeny, tiny Billy Goat Gruff. "I'm not even a snack. Why don't you wait for my middle-sized brother to come along? There's much more meat on him."

"Okay, okay," roared the nasty troll. "Now hurry along before I change my mind."

Later, when the middle-sized Billy Goat Gruff saw his teeny, tiny brother enjoying the green, green grass on the other side of the bridge, he decided to join him.

TRIP, TRAP!

TRIP, TRAP!

TRIP, TRAP!

went his hooves as he tiptoed over the bridge.

But he was only halfway across when...

"ROAR!"

Out jumped the evil troll. "Who's that trip, trapping over my bridge?" he roared.

"Only me," said the middle-sized Billy Goat Gruff. "I'm going to the far meadow to eat green grass. I hope I didn't wake you."

"Oh, no, you don't," roared the nasty troll. "You've disturbed me while I'm fishing, and now I'm going to gobble you up."

"But I'm not very big," said the middle-sized Billy Goat Gruff. " I just have a thick coat. Why don't you wait for my big brother to come along? He's big and fat. He would be a real feast for you."

"All right," roared the troll. "But hurry up before I change my mind."

The big Billy Goat Gruff could hardly believe his eyes when he saw his brothers enjoying the green,

green grass on the other side of the bridge. "They will finish it all if I'm not quick," he thought, as he tiptoed his way across the bridge. But he had barely gone more than a few paces before...

"ROAR!" Out leaped the horrible troll.

"Who's that trip, trapping over my bridge?" roared the troll.

"Just me," said the big Billy Goat Gruff. "I'm on my way to the meadow to eat grass."

"Oh, no, you're not!" roared the troll. "I've heard all about you, and now I'm going to gobble you up."

"Oh, no, you're not," roared the biggest Billy Goat Gruff. Then he lowered his horns and charged!

"Ahhhh!" screamed the nasty troll, as the biggest

Billy Goat Gruff tossed him into the air. "Heeelp!" he screamed, as he flew higher and higher, until, SPLASH, he fell into the deepest part of the river.

Without looking back, the biggest Billy Goat Gruff raced to join his brothers. And from that day on, the three Billy Goats Gruff and all their friends could cross over the bridge to eat the green, green grass whenever they wanted. As for the troll, well, no one ever heard of him again.

One, Two, Three, Four, Five

One, two, three, four, five,
Once I caught a fish alive.
Six, seven, eight, nine, ten,
Then I let it go again.
Why did you let it go?
Because it bit my finger so.
Which finger did it bite?
This little finger on the right.

Itsy Bitsy Spider

Itsy Bitsy spider
Climbed up the water spout;
Down came the rain,
And washed the spider out;
Out came the sun,
And dried up all the rain;
So Itsy Bitsy spider
Climbed up the spout again.

Polly, Put the Kettle On

Polly, put the kettle on,
Polly, put the kettle on,
Polly, put the kettle on,
We'll all have tea.
Sukey, take it off again,
Sukey, take it off again,
Sukey, take it off again,
They've all gone away.

The Gingerbread Man

Once upon a time there lived a little old man and a little old woman. The little old man and the little old woman were very happy, except for one thing—they had no children. So one day they decided to make a child for themselves. They rolled his body out of gingerbread, and used raisins for his eyes and nose, and orange peel for his mouth. Then they put him in the oven to bake.

When the gingerbread child was ready, the little old woman opened the door, and . . . out jumped the Gingerbread Man, and away he ran.

"Come back! Come back!" cried the little old man and the little old woman, running after him as fast as they could. But the Gingerbread Man just laughed, and shouted,

"Run, run as fast as you can.
You can't catch me,
I'm the Gingerbread Man!"

The little old man and the little old woman could not catch him, and soon they gave up. The Gingerbread Man ran on and on, until he met a cow.

"Moo," said the cow. "Stop! I would like to eat you."

"Ha!" said the Gingerbread Man. "I have run away

from a little old man and a little old woman, and now I will run away from you."

The cow began to chase the Gingerbread Man across the field, but the Gingerbread Man simply ran faster, and sang,

"Run, run, as fast as you can. You can't catch me, I'm the Gingerbread Man!"

The cow could not catch him. The Gingerbread Man ran on, until he met a horse.

"Neigh," said the horse. "Stop! I would like to eat you."

"Ha!" said the Gingerbread Man. "I have run away from a little old man, a little old woman, and a cow, and now I will run away from you."

Then the horse began to chase the Gingerbread Man, but the Gingerbread Man ran faster and faster, and as he ran he sang,

"Run, run as fast as you can. You can't catch me, I'm the Gingerbread Man!"

The horse could not catch him, so the Gingerbread Man ran on, until he came to a playground full of children.

"Hey, Gingerbread Man," called the children. "Stop! We would like to eat you."

"Ha!" said the Gingerbread Man. "I have run away from a little old man, a little old woman, a cow, and a horse, and now I will run away from you."

The children began to chase the Gingerbread Man, but it was no use—the Gingerbread Man was just too fast for them.

While he ran he sang,

"Run, run as fast as you can.
You can't catch me,
I'm the Gingerbread Man!"

By now, the Gingerbread Man was feeling very pleased with himself. "No one will ever eat me," he thought, as he came to a river. "I am the smartest person alive."

Just then, a fox appeared and came toward the Gingerbread Man.

"I have run away from a little old man, a little old woman, a cow, a horse, and a playground full of children, and now I will run away from you," shouted the Gingerbread Man.

"Run, run, as fast as you can.
You can't catch me, I'm the Gingerbread Man!"

"I don't want to eat you," laughed the fox. "I just want to help you cross the river. Why don't you jump onto my tail, and I'll carry you across?"

"Okay," said the Gingerbread Man, and up he hopped. When the fox had swum a little way he turned to the Gingerbread Man and said, "My tail is getting tired. Won't you jump onto my back?"

So the Gingerbread Man did.

A little farther on, the fox said to the Gingerbread Man, "You are going to get wet on my back. Won't you jump onto my shoulder?"

So the Gingerbread Man did.

Then, just a bit farther on, the fox said to the Gingerbread Man, "Quickly, my shoulders are sinking. Jump onto my nose. That way you will keep dry."

So the Gingerbread Man did, and before he knew it the fox had flipped the Gingerbread Man up into the air and gulped him down in a single bite.

The poor Gingerbread Man wasn't so smart after all, was he?

The Queen of Hearts

The Queen of Hearts,
She made some tarts
All on a summer's day.

The Knave of Hearts,
He stole the tarts
And took them clean away.

The King of Hearts
Called for the tarts
And beat the Knave full sore.

The Knave of Hearts
Brought back the tarts
And vowed he'd steal no more.

There Was an Old Woman

There was an old woman
who lived in a shoe,
She had so many children
she didn't know what to do;
She gave them some broth
without any bread;
And scolded them soundly
and put them to bed.

Mary, Mary, Quite Contrary

Mary, Mary, quite contrary,
How does your garden grow?
With silver bells and cockle shells
And pretty maids all in a row.

Bobby Shaftoe

Bobby Shaftoe's gone to sea,
Silver buckles on his knee;
He'll come back and marry me,
Pretty Bobby Shaftoe.

This Little Piggy

This little
piggy went
to market,

This little
piggy stayed
at home;

This little
piggy had
roast beef,

And this
little piggy
had none;

And this little piggy cried,
"Wee-wee-wee-wee-wee,"
All the way home.

The Naughty Bears

One sunny summer day, Ben and Peter's mom and dad told them to pack their stuff, because they were going to the beach.

"Yippee!" said Ben. "Can we take our bears?"

"As long as you keep an eye on them," said Daddy. "We don't want to spend all afternoon looking for them if you lose them again!"

Ben and Peter took their teddy bears everywhere they went, but they were always losing them and then there was a great hunt to find them. But the truth was that, when no one was looking, the naughty little bears would run away in search of excitement and adventure.

Today was no different. The family arrived at the

beach and unpacked everything. Daddy sat reading a newspaper and Mommy took out a book. Soon Ben and Peter were busy building sand castles. When the naughty bears saw that no one was looking, they jumped up and ran away, giggling all along the beach.

"Let's go exploring," said Billy, who was the older bear. "I can see a cave over there." He pointed to a dark hole in the rocks close to the water.

"It looks a bit dark and scary," said Bella.

"Don't be silly," said Billy. "You're a bear. Bears like dark caves!"

The little bears clambered over the rocks and into the cave. It was very deep and very dark. Just then, Bella spotted something gleaming on the floor.

She picked it up and showed it to Billy.

"Gold!" said Billy excitedly, taking the little coin from Bella. "This must be a smugglers' cave! Maybe the smugglers are still here. Let's take a look!"

"No!" said Bella. "They could be dangerous. Let's go back." She turned and ran back outside, where she saw to her horror that while they had been exploring, the tide had come in and cut the rocks off from the beach.

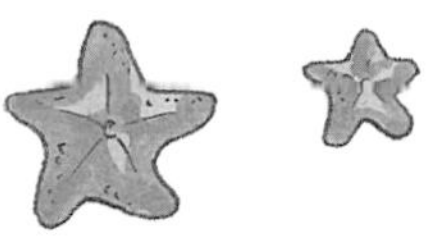

"Billy!" she called. "Come quick, we're stranded!"

Meanwhile, Ben and Peter had finished making sand castles and found that their teddy bears were missing.

"Oh, no," groaned Daddy. "Not again!"

The family hunted high and low along the beach, but there was no sign of the bears. "Maybe they've been washed out to sea," said Peter, his voice trembling at the thought.

Back at the cave, the naughty bears could see their owners looking for them. They jumped up and down and waved their paws.

"It's no use," said Bella, "they can't see us. We're too small."

"Don't worry," said Billy, trying to sound braver than he felt.

Just then, two men appeared from the other side of the rocks. The bears froze—these must be the smugglers! They trembled in fear as the men picked them up, clambered over the rocks, and tossed them into a little boat that had been hidden from view. The bears clung

together at the bottom of the boat as the men jumped in and began to row. Where were they taking them?

After a while, the boat stopped and one of the men jumped out. He grabbed the bears and held them in the air high above his head, calling out, "Has anyone lost these bears?"

Everyone on the beach looked up, and Ben and Peter

raced over and grabbed their bears.

"Thank you," said Daddy. "We've been looking everywhere for them."

"We found them up by that cave," said one of the men, pointing over to the cave. "Your kids must have left them there."

"But they've been here building sand castles all afternoon..." said Daddy, looking puzzled...

No one ever did find out how the naughty bears had gotten to the cave, or where the little coin in Billy's pocket came from. But from then on Daddy said the bears had to stay at home. The naughty bears didn't really mind. They'd had enough adventures for the time being. And it gave them lots of time to play their favorite game—hide-and-seek!

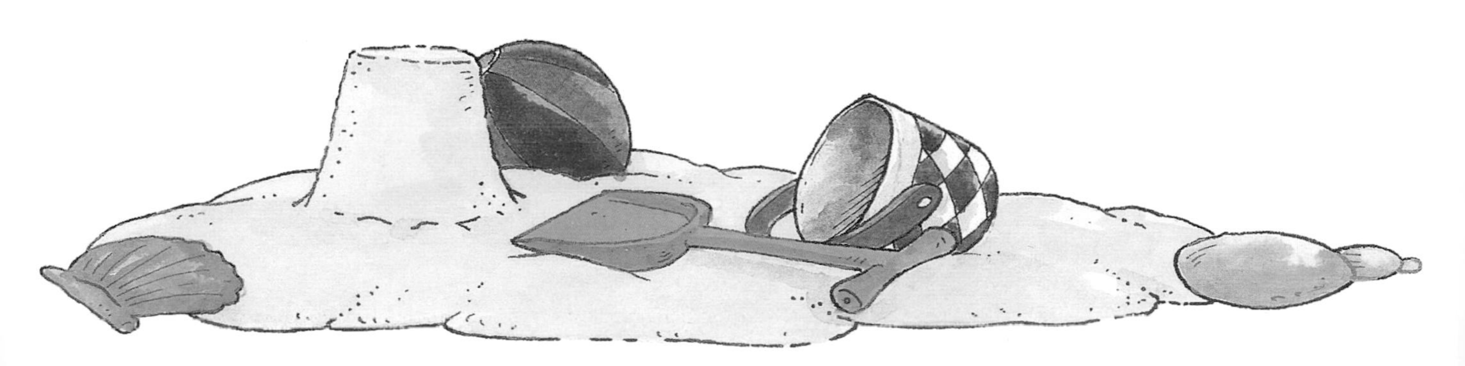

Ten Little Teddy Bears

Ten little teddy bears, standing in a line,
One of them went fishing, so then there were nine.

Nine little teddy bears, marching through a gate,
One stopped to tie his shoe, so then there were eight.

Eight little teddy bears, floating up in heaven,
One fell down and broke his crown,
so then there were seven.

Seven little teddy bears, doing magic tricks,
One made himself disappear, so then there were six.

Six little teddy bears, about to take a dive,
One of them was scared of heights,
so then there were five.

Five little teddy bears, running on the shore,
One went surfing in the waves,
so then there were four.

Four little teddy bears, having cake and tea,
One of them was feeling sick,
so then there were three.

Three little teddy bears, heading for the zoo,
One thought he'd take the bus,
so then there were two.

Two little teddy bears, playing in the sun,
One of them got sunburned, so then there was one.

One little teddy bear, who's had lots of fun,
It's time for him to go to sleep,
so now there are none.

Lazy Mary

Lazy Mary will you get up,
Will you get up, will you get up?
Lazy Mary will you get up,
Will you get up today?

Six o'clock and you're still sleeping,
Daylight's creeping o'er your windowsill.

Lazy Mary will you get up,
Will you get up, will you get up?
Lazy Mary will you get up,
Will you get up today?

Seven o'clock and you're still snoring,
Sunshine's pouring through your window pane.

Lazy Mary will you get up,
Will you get up, will you get up?
Lazy Mary will you get up,
Will you get up today?

Eight o'clock, you've missed your train,
Can you explain why you're still in your bed?

Lucy Locket

Lucy Locket lost her pocket,
Kitty Fisher found it.
Not a penny was there in it,
Only ribbon round it.

Cinderella's umbrella's
Full of holes all over.
Every time it starts to rain
She has to run for cover.

Aladdin's lamp is getting damp,
And is no longer gleaming.
It doesn't spark when it's dark,
But it just won't stop steaming.

Nippy Snippy

Eeeny, meeny, miney, mo,
Here comes Crab to pinch your toe!
Shout out loud and he'll let go—
Eeeny, meeny, miney, mo!

Nippy, snippy, snappy, snip,
Be careful when you take a dip,
Or Crab will catch you in his grip!
Nippy, snippy, snappy, snip!

Whale Song

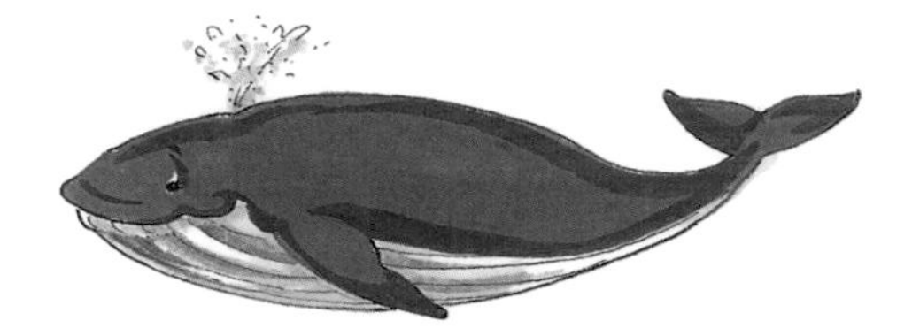

"Oh, what a beautiful morning!"

sang Flippy the whale, as streaks of sunlight filtered down through the clear blue ocean. He swam to and fro, twirled around, then whooshed up through the waves and jumped clear of the water in a perfect pirouette.

Flippy loved to sing and dance. The trouble was, although he was a very graceful dancer, his singing was terrible! His big mouth would open wide, as he boomed out song after song—but none of them were in tune! The dreadful sound echoed through the ocean for miles, sending all the

fish and other ocean creatures diving into the rocks and reefs for cover, as the waters shook around them. It was always worse when the sun shone, because the bright warm sun made Flippy want to sing and dance with happiness. It had gotten so bad that the other creatures had begun to pray for dull skies and rain.

"Something has to be done!" complained Wobble the jellyfish. "Flippy's booming voice makes me quiver and shake so much that I can't see where I'm going!"

"Well, I know where I'm going," said Snappy the lobster. "As far away as possible. My head is splitting from Flippy's awful wailing."

"Someone will have to tell Flippy not to sing anymore," said Sparky the stingray.

"But it will hurt his feelings," said Wobble.

"Not as much as his singing hurts my ears!" snapped Snappy.

And so they decided that Sparky would tell Flippy the next day that they did not want him to sing any more songs. Wobble was right. Flippy was very upset when he heard that the others did not like his singing. He cried big, salty tears.

"I was only trying to enjoy myself!" he sobbed. "I didn't realize I was upsetting everyone else."

"There, there," said Sparky, wishing he had not been chosen to give the little whale the bad news. "You can still enjoy dancing."

"It's not the same without music," said Flippy miserably. "You can't get the rhythm." And he swam off into the deep waters, saying he wanted to be alone for a while.

As Flippy lay on the bottom of the ocean, feeling

very sorry for himself, a beautiful sound came floating through the water from far away in the distance. It sounded like someone singing. Flippy wanted to know who was making such a lovely sound, so with a flick of his big tail, he set off in the direction it was coming from.

As he got closer, he could hear a soft voice singing a beautiful melody. Peering out from behind a big rock, he saw that the voice belonged to a little octopus, who was shuffling and swaying on the ocean floor. His legs seemed to be going in all directions, as he stumbled and tripped along. Then he tried to spin around, but his legs got tangled and he crashed to the ground in a heap.

"Oh, dear," said Leggy the octopus. "I seem to have eight left feet!"

Flippy looked out shyly from behind the rock.

"What are you trying to do?" he asked.

The little octopus looked kind of embarrassed.

"I was trying to dance," he said, blushing pink. "But I'm not very good at it."

"Well, maybe I could teach you," said Flippy. "I'm a very good dancer. And in return, there is something that I would like you to teach me..."

A few weeks later, Wobble, Snappy, and Sparky were discussing how they missed having Flippy around, when they heard a strange and beautiful sound floating toward them through the ocean.

"Oh, what a beautiful morning..."

came the song, only this time there were two voices singing in perfect harmony!

"That can't possibly be Flippy!" said the others in surprise. But to their amazement, as the voices came closer they saw that, sure enough, it was Flippy, spinning and twirling as he danced gracefully toward them with his new friend!

My Best Friend

He cuddles me at bedtime,
And keeps me safe at night,
If I have a bad dream,
And wake up in a fright.

He is my constant playmate,
And often shares my treats.
He always lets me win our games,
And his smile just can't be beat.

I tell him all my secrets,
And he never shows surprise.
He listens to my problems,
With kindness in his eyes.

And when I'm feeling lonely,
On him I can depend,
He's more than just a teddy bear,
He is my best, best friend!

Some Teddy Bears

Some teddy bears are tiny,
Some teddy bears are tall,
Some teddy bears are big and round,
And some teddy bears are small.

Some teddy bears are woolly,
Some teddy bears are rough,
Some teddy bears have shaggy fur,
And some are balls of fluff.

Some teddy bears look happy,
Some teddy bears look sad,
Some teddy bears are very good,
And some teddy bears are bad.

But all teddy bears are loyal,
And all teddy bears are true,
And all teddy bears need lots of love
And hugs from me and you.

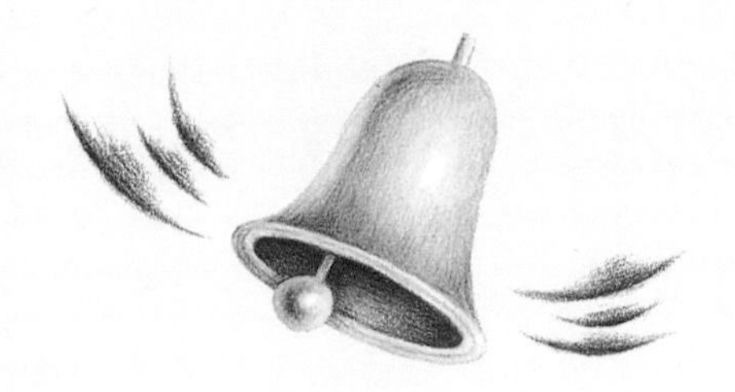

Ding Dong Bell

Ding dong bell,
Pussy's in the well!
Who put her in?
Little Johnny Green.
Who pulled her out?
Little Tommy Trout.
What a naughty boy was that,
To try to drown poor pussy cat,
Who never did any harm,
But killed the mice in his father's barn.

Lazy Teddy

There was nothing Lazy Teddy liked more than to be tucked up snug and warm in Joshua's bed. Every morning the alarm clock would ring and Joshua would leap out of bed and fling open the curtains. "I love mornings!" he'd say, stretching his arms up high as the sun poured in through the window. "You're crazy!" Teddy would mutter, and he'd burrow down beneath the quilt to the bottom of the bed, where he'd spend the rest of the morning snoozing happily.

"Come out and play, you lazy bear," Joshua would call. But Lazy Teddy wouldn't budge. He would just snore even louder.

Joshua wished that Teddy would be more lively, like his other friends' bears. He loved having adventures, but they would be even better if Teddy would share them with him.

One evening, Joshua decided to have a talk with Teddy before they went to bed. He told him all about the fishing trip he'd been on that day with his friends and their teddy bears.

"It was lots of fun, Teddy. I wish you'd been there. It really is time you stopped being such a lazybones. Tomorrow is my birthday, and I'm having a party. There will be games, and gifts, and ice cream. Please promise you'll come?"

"It does sound like fun," said Teddy. "Okay, I promise. I'll get up

just this once."

The next morning, Joshua was up bright and early. "Yippee, it's my birthday today!" he yelled, dancing around the room. He pulled the covers off his bed. "Come on, Teddy, time to get up!"

"Just five more minutes!" groaned Teddy, and he rolled over and went straight back to sleep. When Joshua came back up to his room after breakfast, Teddy still wasn't up. Well, by now Joshua was getting very annoyed with Teddy. He reached over and poked him in the tummy. Teddy opened one eye and growled. "Wake up, Teddy! You promised, remember?" said Joshua.

Teddy yawned. "Oh, all right!" he said, and, muttering and grumbling, he climbed out of bed. He washed his face and paws, brushed his teeth, and put on his best red vest.

"There, I'm ready!" he said.

"Good," said Joshua. "It's about time!"

Just then the doorbell rang, and Joshua ran to answer it. "I'll come and get you in a minute," he said to Teddy. But when he returned there was no sign of Teddy, just gentle snoring coming from the bottom of the bed.

Joshua was so angry and upset with Lazy Teddy that he decided to leave him right where he was. "He'll just have to miss the party!" he said. Deep down though, he was hurt that Teddy hadn't kept his promise.

Joshua enjoyed his party, although he wished that Teddy had been there. That night when he got into bed, he lay crying quietly into his pillow.

Teddy lay awake in the dark, listening. He knew Joshua was crying because he had let him down, and he felt very ashamed of himself.

"I'm sorry!" whispered Lazy Teddy, and he snuggled up to Joshua and stroked him with a paw until he fell asleep.

The next morning when the alarm clock rang, Joshua leaped out of bed as usual. But what was going on? Teddy had leaped out of

bed too, and was stretching his paws up high. Joshua looked at him in amazement.

"Well, what are we doing today?" asked Teddy.

"Ha... ha... having a picnic," stammered Joshua, surprised. "Are you coming?"

"Of course," said Teddy. And from that day on, Teddy was up bright and early every day, ready to enjoy another day of adventures with Joshua, and he never let him down again.

If You're Happy and You Know It

If you're happy and you know it,
Clap your hands.
If you're happy and you know it,
Clap your hands.
If you're happy and you know it,
And you really want to show it,
If you're happy and you know it,
Clap your hands.

If you're happy and you know it,
Nod your head, etc.

If you're happy and you know it,
Stamp your feet, etc.

If you're happy and you know it,
Say "Ha, ha!" etc.

If you're happy and you know it,
Do all four!

Elephants Never Forget

I woke up this morning, astounded,
To find my long trunk in a knot!
I know it must be to remind me
To remember something I forgot!

But though I've been thinking all morning
I haven't remembered it yet.
Still, I'm sure I will think of it soon,
Because elephants never forget!

Itchy Spots

Poor Monkey was wriggling
And jiggling around,
Scratching and making
A chattering sound.

"They're driving me mad,
Someone help me please—
I have to get rid of
These terrible fleas!"

Then along came a bear
In a bit of a stew—
"I've got such a bad itch,
I don't know what to do!

"It's right in a spot
I can't reach with my paws.
So why not scratch my back,
And I will scratch yours!"

Teddy Bears' Picnic

Little Bear brought chocolate cake,
Raggy Bear brought honey,
Baby Bear brought ice cream,
With butterscotch all runny!

Tough Old Ted brought cupcakes,
Silky Bear brought jello,
Shaggy Bear brought cookies and
Egg sandwiches all yellow!

Off they went into the woods,
A sunny spot they found,
And had a teddy bears' picnic,
As they passed the treats around!

Little Dog Lost

"Brrr," shivered Scruffy. "It's cold tonight."

"Well, snuggle up closer to me," said his mom.

"It's not fair," Scruffy grumbled. "Why do we have to sleep outside in the cold? The cats are allowed to sleep inside, in nice warm baskets!"

"We're farm dogs, dear," said Mom. "We have to be tough, and work hard to earn our keep."

"I'd rather be a cat," mumbled Scruffy. "All they do is wash themselves, eat, and sleep."

"We don't have such a bad life," said Mom. "Now stop feeling sorry for yourself, and get some rest. We've got a lot of work to do tomorrow."

The next day, Scruffy woke early and trotted down the o path for a walk. He ran through the grass, chasing rabbits and sniffing at the flowers.

Now, usually when he got to the end of the path he stopped and turned back. But today he saw a big red truck parked outside a house there. The back of the truck was open, and Scruffy thought he would just climb inside and take a look.

The truck was full of furniture. At the back was a big armchair with soft pillows. Scruffy clambered onto it. “I could doze all day, like a cat!” he told himself. He closed his eyes and before he knew it he had fallen fast asleep.

Scruffy awoke some time later with a sharp jolt.

“Oh, no, I fell asleep!” he groaned. “I’d better hurry back. We’ve got a busy day ahead!”

But then he saw that the truck doors were closed!

He could hear voices outside.

"Oh, no! I'll be in trouble if they find me in here," thought Scruffy, and he hid behind the chair.

The back of the truck opened, and Scruffy peered out. Two men started unloading the furniture.

When Scruffy was sure that no one was looking, he crept out of the truck, but he was no longer in the countryside where he lived! He was in a big, noisy town, full of buildings and cars.

Poor Scruffy had no idea where he was!

"The truck must have carried me away," thought Scruffy, feeling frightened.

All day long, Scruffy roamed around trying to find his way home, feeling cold, tired, and hungry. At last he lay down and began to howl miserably.

"What's the matter, pup?" he heard a man's kind

voice say. "You look lost. Come home with me." Scruffy gave the man's hand a grateful lick, then jumped up and followed him home.

When they arrived at the man's house Scruffy sat on the doorstep, hoping the man might bring out some food for him to eat. But the man said, "Come on in—you can't stay out there."

Scruffy followed the man in, and found a little poodle waiting to meet him. Scruffy stared at her in amazement. What had happened to her fur?

"You'd better have a bath before supper," said the man, looking at Scruffy's dirty white coat. The man washed him in a big tub, then brushed his tangled coat. Scruffy howled miserably. What had he done to deserve such punishment?

"Don't you like it?" asked the poodle shyly.

"No, I don't," said Scruffy. "All this washing and cleaning is for cats!"

Next the man gave them supper—small bowls of dry pellets. Scruffy sniffed at them in disgust. He was used to chunks of meat and a nice big bone.

"This looks like cat food," said Scruffy miserably. After supper the poodle climbed into a big basket in the kitchen.

"I thought that belonged to a cat," said Scruffy. He tried sleeping in the basket, but he was hot and uncomfortable. He missed counting the stars to help him fall asleep, and most of all he missed his mom. "I want to go home," he cried, and big tears slipped down his nose.

The next day, the man put a leash on Scruffy and took him into town. He hated being dragged along and not being able to sniff at things.

Then, as they crossed the main street, Scruffy heard a familiar bark, and saw his mom's head hanging out of the window of the farmer's truck! He started to howl, dragged the man over to where the truck was parked, then leaped up at the window, barking excitedly. The farmer could hardly believe it was Scruffy—he had never seen him so clean! The man explained how he had found Scruffy, and the farmer thanked the man for taking such good care of him.

On the way back home, Scruffy told his mom all about his adventure and what had happened.

"I thought you had run away because you didn't like being a farm dog," she said gently.

"Oh, no, Mom," said Scruffy quickly. "I love being a farm dog. I can't wait to get home to a nice big juicy bone and our little bed beneath the stars!"

Round and Round the Garden

Round and round
the garden,
Like a teddy bear;

One step, two steps,
Tickle you under there!

Round and round
the haystack,
Went the little mouse.

One step, two steps,
Into his little house.

The Bear Will Have to Go

While Lucy slept in the shade of a tree, Cuthbert went for a walk into the woods and soon got lost. He had no idea how to get back, so he sat down and thought about what to do next.

When Lucy woke up, she looked around in surprise. Her teddy bear, Cuthbert, was missing. She thought someone had taken him, for she didn't know that when people are asleep their teddy bears like to go walking.

"Cuthbert!" she called. "Cuthbert, where are you?" He wasn't very far away. Lucy soon found him sniffing at a clump of moss.

"There you are!" she sighed. "I thought I'd lost you.

"There you are!" she sighed. "I thought I'd lost you. Where's your vest?"

In fact, Lucy really had lost Cuthbert, for the bear she was taking home was not a teddy bear at all, but a real baby bear cub! As they ran back through the woods, the bear in Lucy's arms kept very still.

Soon they were back in Lucy's bedroom. Lucy flung the bear onto her bed, then went to run a bath.

"Time to escape!" thought the bear. He slid off the bed, pulling the covers after him. He ran over to the window and tried to climb up the drapes. They tore and tumbled into a heap on the floor.

Just then Lucy's mother came into the room. The bear froze. Then Lucy appeared.

"Look at this mess," said Lucy's mother. "You've been playing with that bear again. Please tidy up."

Lucy had no idea how her room had gotten so messy, but she tidied up, took the bear into the bathroom, and put him on the edge of the tub.

"Don't fall in," she said and went to get a towel. The bear jumped into the tub with a big splash. He waved his paws wildly, sending sprays of soapy water across the room. When he heard footsteps, he froze and floated on his back in the water as if nothing was wrong. It was Lucy, followed by her mother.

"Oh, Lucy! What a mess!" cried her mother.

"Cuthbert must have fallen in," cried Lucy, rubbing his wet fur with a towel.

"A teddy bear couldn't make all this mess on its own," said Lucy's mother. "Please clean it up."

Lucy looked carefully at Cuthbert. Something was different about him, but she just couldn't figure out what it was.

That night, while Lucy slept, the bear tiptoed downstairs. He needed to get back to the woods where he belonged, but he was hungry.

When Lucy came down for a glass of milk she found him with food all over his paws. The bear froze. Then her mother appeared in the doorway.

"This is the last straw, Lucy," said her mother angrily. "You have really misbehaved today, and every time something happens you've got that bear with you. If there is any more bad behavior, the bear will have to go."

When her mother had gone back upstairs, Lucy looked carefully at the bear.

"You're not Cuthbert, are you?" she said. The bear looked back at her and blinked. Lucy gasped. "You're a real bear!"

Now all the mess made sense! Lucy could hardly believe she had made such a mistake. She stroked the bear gently and he licked her finger.

"I'd better get you back to the woods

before there's any more trouble," she said. "And I'd better try to find the real Cuthbert."

So early next morning, before her parents were awake, she crept out of the house carrying the bear. Out in the woods she put the bear on the ground. He licked her hand and padded away.

Lucy was sad to see the little bear go. She wiped a tear from her eye as she turned away... and there at the foot of a tree sat her teddy bear, Cuthbert! Lucy picked him up and hugged him.

"Where have you been?" she asked. "You'll never believe how much trouble I got into! What have you been doing all night?"

Cuthbert said nothing. He just smiled. What had he been doing all night? Well, that's another story!

In a Spin

I had a little teddy bear,
He went everywhere with me,
But now I've gone and lost him,
Oh, where can my bear be?

I've looked behind the sofa,
I've looked beneath the bed,
I've looked out in the garden,
And even in the shed!

I've looked inside the bathtub,
And underneath my chair,
Oh, where, oh, where is Teddy?
I've hunted everywhere!

At last I try the kitchen,
My face breaks in a grin.
Teddy's in the washing machine—
Mom sent him for a spin!

There Was a Crooked Man

There was a crooked man
And he walked a crooked mile;
He found a crooked sixpence
Against a crooked stile.
He brought a crooked cat
Which caught a crooked mouse,
And they all lived together
In a little crooked house.

Knick Knack Paddy Whack

This old man, he played one,
He played knick knack on my drum.
With a knick knack paddy whack,
give a dog a bone,
This old man went rolling home.

This old man, he played two,
He played knick knack on my shoe.
With a knick knack paddy whack,
give a dog a bone,
This old man went rolling home.

This old man, he played three,
He played knick knack on my knee.
With a knick knack paddy whack,
give a dog a bone,
This old man went rolling home.

This old man, he played four,
He played knick knack on my door.
With a knick knack paddy whack,
give a dog a bone,
This old man went rolling home.

This old man, he played five,
He played knick knack on my hive.
With a knick knack paddy whack,
give a dog a bone,
This old man went rolling home.

The Littlest Pig

Little Pig had a secret. He snuggled down in the warm hay with his brothers and sisters, looked up at the dark sky twinkling with stars, and smiled a secret smile to himself. Maybe it wasn't so bad being the littlest pig after all.

Not so long ago, Little Pig had been feeling really annoyed. He was the youngest and by far the smallest pig in the family. He had five brothers and five sisters and they were all much bigger and fatter than he was. The farmer's wife called him Runt, because he was the smallest pig of the litter.

"I don't think little Runt will amount to much," she told her friend Daisy, as they stopped by to bring the piglets some fresh hay.

His brothers and sisters teased him terribly. "Poor little Runtie," they said to him, giggling. "You must be the smallest pig in the world!"

"Leave me alone!" said Little Pig, and he crept off to the corner of the pig pen, where he curled into a ball and started to cry. "If you weren't all so greedy and let me have some food, maybe I'd be bigger!" he mumbled sadly.

Every feeding time was the same—the others all pushed and shoved, and shunted Little Pig out of the way, until all that was left were the scraps. He would never grow bigger at this rate.

Then one day Little Pig made an important discovery. He was hiding in the corner of the pen, as usual, when he spied a little hole in the fence hidden away behind the feeding trough.

"I think I could fit through there!" thought Little Pig excitedly.

He waited all day until it was time for bed and then, when he was sure that all of his brothers and sisters were fast asleep, he wriggled through the hole. Suddenly he was outside, free to go wherever he pleased. And what an adventure he had!

First he ran to the henhouse and gobbled up the bowls of grain. Then he ran to the field, slipped under the fence, and crunched up Donkey's carrots.

He ran into the vegetable patch and munched a whole row of cabbages. What a wonderful feast! Then, when his little belly was full to bursting, he headed for home. On the way he stopped beside the hedge. What was that lovely smell? He rooted around until he found where it was coming from—it was a bank of wild strawberries.

Little Pig had never tasted anything so delicious.

"Tomorrow night, I'll start with these!" he promised himself as he trotted back home to the pigpen.

Quietly he wriggled back through the hole, and soon fell fast asleep snuggled up against his mother, smiling contentedly.

Night after night Little Pig continued his tasty adventures, creeping out through the hole when the others were sleeping. He no longer minded when they pushed him out of the way at feeding time, because he knew that a much better feast awaited him outside. Sometimes he would find the farm dog's bowl filled with scraps from the farmer's supper, or buckets of oats ready for the horses. "Yum, yum—piggy oatmeal!" he would giggle as he gobbled it up.

But as the days and weeks went by, and Little Pig grew bigger and fatter, it was more of a squeeze to wriggle through the hole each night.

Little Pig knew that soon he would no longer be able to fit through the hole, but by then he would be big enough to stand up to his brothers and sisters. And for now he was enjoying his secret!

Achoo!

Mouse's eyes filled up with water,
His little nose started to twitch,
A tingling tickled his whiskers,
And then his knees started to itch.

He got a bad case of the hiccups,
Then threw back his head in a sneeze,
And he said, "I'm feeling really bad,
Because I'm allergic to cheese!"

Giddyup, Teddy

Giddyup, Teddy,
Don't you stop!
Ride on the
hobbyhorse,
Clippety clop!
Clippety clopping,
Round and round.
Giddyup,
We're toybox bound!

Three Bears in a Tub

Rub-a-dub, dub,
Three bears in a tub,
Sailing across the sea!
But the smell of hotcakes,
And other nice bakes,
Will bring them back
home to me!

Midnight Fun

Just as midnight's striking,
When everyone's asleep,
Teddy bears yawn and stretch and
shake,
And out of warm beds creep.

They sneak out from their houses,
And gather in the dark,
Then skip along the empty streets,

Heading for the park.
And there beneath the moonlight,
They tumble down the slides,
They swoosh up high upon the swings,
And play on all the rides.

And when the sun comes peeping,
They rush home to their beds,
And just as children all wake up,
They become sleepyheads!

Birthday Bunnies

"It's my first birthday tomorrow!" announced Snowy, a little white rabbit, very proudly. "Isn't that exciting?"

"Yes, very exciting!" said Whiskers, her brother. "Because it's my birthday, too!"

"And mine!" said Patch.

"And mine!" said Nibble.

"And mine!" said Twitch.

"Do you think Mom and Dad have a surprise for us?" asked Snowy.

"I hope so!" said Whiskers.

"Me too!" said Patch.

"Me too!" said Nibble.

"Me too!" said Twitch.

Mrs. Rabbit was listening outside the door as her

children were getting ready for bed. She heard the little bunnies chattering excitedly about their birthdays the next day.

What could she do to make it a special day for them? She sat and thought very hard, and later that evening, when Mr. Rabbit came home, she said: "It's the children's first birthday tomorrow, and I'm planning a surprise for them. I want to make them a carrot cake, but I will need some carrots. Could you go and dig up some nice fresh ones from your vegetable patch?"

"Certainly, dear," said Mr. Rabbit, and he went right back outside.

Mr. Rabbit was proud of the carrots he grew. They were very fine carrots, crunchy and sweet and

delicious. Every year he entered them in the County Fair, and they almost always won first prize. So you can imagine his dismay when he arrived at his vegetable patch to find that every single carrot had been dug up and stolen!

He marched back inside. "Someone has stolen my carrots!" he announced to his wife angrily. "And I am going to find out just who it is!"

And although it was getting late, he went back outside and set off to find the culprit.

First he stopped at Hungry Hare's house and knocked at the door.

"Someone has stolen my carrots!" Mr. Rabbit said. "Do you know who?"

"Oh, yes," said Hungry Hare. "But it wasn't me."

And although Mr. Rabbit kept asking him, Hungry Hare would say no more.

Next Mr. Rabbit went to Sly Fox's house.

"Someone has stolen my carrots!" he said. "Do you know who?"

"Oh, yes," said Sly Fox. "But it wasn't me." And although Mr. Rabbit begged and pleaded with him, Sly Fox would say no more.

So Mr. Rabbit marched to Bill Badger's house, and asked if he knew who had taken the carrots.

"Why, yes, in fact, I do," said Bill Badger. "But it wasn't me."

And just like the others, he would say no more. It was the same wherever Mr. Rabbit went, and although he got very angry, and stamped his foot, no one would tell him who had stolen his carrots!

"You'll find out soon enough," said Red Squirrel.

So Mr. Rabbit went home feeling very puzzled.

"It seems that everyone knows who it was, but no

one will tell me!" said Mr. Rabbit to his wife.

"Not everyone, dear," she said. "I don't know who it was either. All I know is that it's our children's first birthday tomorrow, and we have no surprise for them." And feeling very miserable and confused, they went to bed, determined to get to the bottom of the mystery in the morning.

Next day the little bunnies came running into the kitchen, where their parents were having breakfast.

"Happy birthday, everyone!" called Snowy.

"Happy birthday!" cried the other little bunnies.

"Now, it's not much, but I wanted to give each of you a surprise!" Snowy went on. "By the way, I hope you don't mind, Dad." And with that Snowy pulled

out a box of juicy carrots, each tied with a bow, and handed one to each of her brothers and sisters.

"Hey!" cried Whiskers, "I had exactly the same

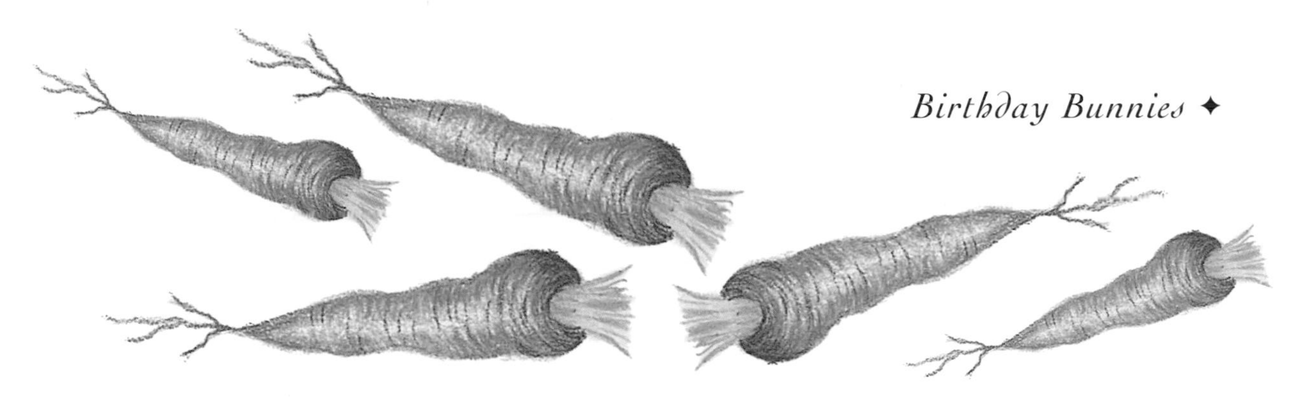

idea!" and he pulled out another box of carrots.

"Me too!" said Patch.

"Me too!" said Nibble.

"Me too!" said Twitch.

Soon there was a huge pile of juicy carrots heaped on the kitchen table.

"So that's what happened to my carrots!" cried Mr. Rabbit in amazement. "I thought they had been stolen!" And when he told the little bunnies the story they laughed till their sides ached. Then Mrs. Rabbit put on her apron and shooed them outside.

"Just leave the carrots with me," she said. "I have a birthday surprise of my own in store!"

And so the mystery was solved. It turned out that Hungry Hare had seen the little bunnies creep out one by one, and each dig up a few carrots when they thought no one was looking. He knew it was their birthdays and he guessed what they were doing. He had told the other forest folk, and everyone thought it was a great joke.

Mr. Rabbit felt very ashamed that he had been so angry with everyone, when they were really just keeping the secret. To apologize, he invited them for a special birthday lunch, which the little bunnies thought was a great surprise.

And of course the highlight of the day was when Mrs. Rabbit appeared from the kitchen carrying—what else?—an enormous carrot cake!

Jack Be Nimble

Jack be nimble,
Jack be quick,
Jack jump over
The candlestick.

Happy Hippopotamus

Hey! Look at me,
A happy hippopotamus,
Covered in mud
From my head to my bottom-us!
Squishing and squelching
And making an awful fuss,
Rolling around in my bath!

I like to blow bubbles,
Breathe out through my nose-es,
To wriggle and jiggle
The mud through my toes-es,
And would you believe it
That I smell like roses,
When I come out of my bath!

To the tune of "Oh, Dear, What Can the Matter Be?"

Boys and Girls, Come Out to Play

Boys and girls, come out to play,
The moon doth shine as bright as day.
Leave your supper and leave your sleep,
And meet your playfellows in the street.
Come with a whoop and come with a call,
Come with a good will or not at all.

Up the ladder and down the wall,
A halfpenny loaf will serve us all.
You find milk, and I'll find flour,
And we'll have a pudding in half an hour.

Tea with the Queen

Teddy bear, teddy bear,
Where have you been?
I've been to London
To visit the queen!

I went to her palace,
And knocked at the gate,
And one of her soldiers said,
"Will you please wait?"

Then one of her footmen,
All dressed in red,
Led me inside, saying,
"Step this way, Ted!"

And there in a huge room,
High on her throne,
Sat the poor queen,
Drinking tea all alone.

She said, "How delightful,
Sit down, fill your tum!"
And soon we were chatting
Just like old friends!

And when time came to leave,
She shook hands and then,
She said, "Do come back soon,
We must do this again!"

Barney the Boastful Bear

Barney was a very boastful bear. "Look at my lovely soft fur!" he would say to the other toys. "See how it shines!"

Barney loved to talk about himself. "I'm the smartest toy in the playroom!" he would say. "It's a well-known fact."

He didn't know that the other toys all laughed about him behind his back.

"That bear thinks he's so smart," growled Scotty Dog. "But he isn't smart enough to know when everyone's sick of him!"

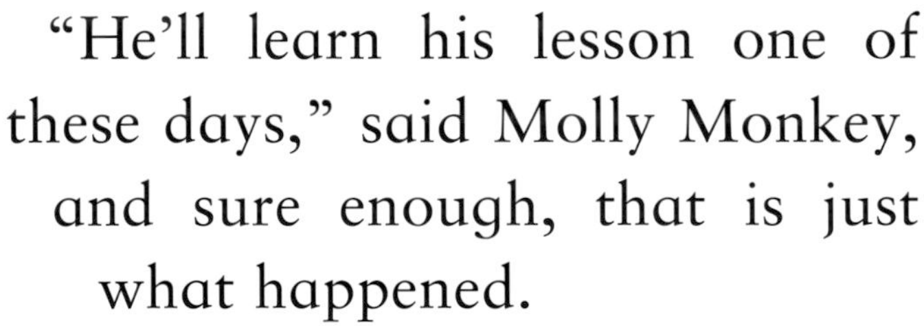

"He'll learn his lesson one of these days," said Molly Monkey, and sure enough, that is just what happened.

One hot summer day, the

toys lazed in the warm playroom. "Wouldn't it be nice if we could go for a walk outside?" said Rag Doll.

"Maybe we could even have a picnic in the woods!" said Old Bear.

"Even better, we could go for a drive in the toy car first!" said Rabbit.

"But none of us is big enough or smart enough to drive the toy car," said Rag Doll sadly.

"I am!" came a voice from the corner. It was Barney. He had been listening to them talking. "I can drive the toy car. And I know the best place for a picnic in the woods," he said.

"We've never seen you drive the car," said Rabbit suspiciously.

"That's because I drive it at night, when you're asleep," said Barney. "I'm a very good driver, in fact."

"Ooh, then let's go!" cried Rag Doll. And in no time at all they had packed a picnic and were ready and waiting in the car.

"Um, I don't really feel like driving today," mumbled Barney. "It's too hot."

But the others were not interested in hearing excuses, so Barney reluctantly climbed into the driver's seat and started the engine. You see, the truth was that Barney had never really driven the car before, and he was scared. But he wanted to show off, so he pretended to know what he was doing.

Off they went down the garden path. "Toot, toot!" Barney beeped the horn as he turned the little car out

into the country path, and soon they were driving along, singing merrily.

All was going well, until Rag Doll suddenly said, "Hey, Barney, didn't we just miss the turn-off for the woods?"

"I know where I'm going," said Barney angrily. "Leave it to me." And he made the little car go faster.

" Hey, slow down, Barney!" called Old Bear from the back seat. "My fur is getting all ruffled." He was starting to feel anxious.

"I don't need a backseat driver, thank you," said Barney with a growl, and he made the car go even faster. By now the others were starting to feel scared, but Barney was having a great time.

"Aren't I a wonderful driver!" he chuckled. "Look—no hands!" And he took his paws off the steering wheel. Just then they reached a sharp corner. The little car went spinning off the side of the road and crashed into a tree, dumping all the toys out into the ditch!

They were a bit dazed, but luckily no one was hurt. They were not pleased with Barney, though.

"You silly bear!" said Rabbit angrily. "We could all have been badly hurt!"

"We'll have to walk home now," said Rag Doll, rubbing her head. "Where are we?"

Everyone looked at Barney.

"Don't ask me!" he said quietly.

"But you said you knew the way!" said Old Bear indignantly.

"I was only pretending," said Barney, his voice trembling. "I don't really know how to drive, and I don't know where we are!" And he started to cry.

The other toys were furious with Barney.

"You naughty boastful bear!" they scolded. "Now look at the trouble your boasting has gotten us into!"

The lost toys walked through the dark woods all night long, clinging together in fright as shadows loomed around them.

They had never been out at night before. Then, just before dawn, they spotted the little house where they lived, and crept back into the playroom. What a relief it was to be home again!

Luckily their owner had not noticed that they were missing, so she never knew what an adventure her toys had been having while she was fast asleep. She often wondered what had happened to her toy car, though.

As for Barney, he was very sorry for the trouble he had caused. After a while the other toys forgave him, and he never boasted about anything again.

Pop Goes the Weasel

Half a pound of tuppenny rice,
Half a pound of treacle.
That's the way the money goes,
POP! goes the weasel.

Two Little Men in a Flying Saucer

Two little men in a flying saucer
Flew round the world one day.

They looked to the left and right a bit,
And couldn't bear the sight of it,

And then they flew away.

There Was an Old Woman Tossed Up in a Blanket

There was an old woman tossed up in a blanket,
Seventeen times as high as the moon;
But where she was going, no mortal could tell it
For under her arm, she carried a broom.

"Old woman, old woman, old woman," said I,
"Whither, ah whither, ah whither so high?"
"To sweep the cobwebs from the sky."
"May I come with you?" "Aye, by and by."

The Ugly Duckling

It was a beautiful summer day. The sun shone brightly on Mother Duck as she laid her eggs. "Quack, quack," she went, as she stood up to count the eggs. "Gosh, that egg is a really big one," she thought. "It will probably turn out to be a big strong drake, like Father Duck." Happy, she settled back down on her nest.

Mother Duck had been sitting on her eggs for a long time when suddenly,

CR . . . ACK

CR . . . ACK, the eggs began to hatch. One by one, the yellow ducklings appeared. Soon Mother Duck had four beautiful, fluffy babies. Now only the really big egg was left.

Mother Duck sat patiently on the really big egg until, at last, CR . . . ACK, out burst a duckling. But my, what an ugly duckling it was! It was large and gray, and not at all beautiful like the others. "Hmmm," thought Mother Duck, "perhaps it isn't a duckling after all. I'll take it to the water and see."

"Follow me," called Mother Duck. One, two, three, four, five . . . the ducklings hurried after her. SPLASH! She jumped into the river.

"Quack, quack!" she called out, and all the ducklings splashed into the water. Soon all of them, even the ugly gray one, were swimming along.

Next, Mother Duck introduced her babies to the other ducks around the barnyard. "Now, my dears," she said quietly, "bow your heads and say 'quack' to the Old Duck."

All the ducklings, even the ugly gray one, did as they were told. But the other ducks just laughed when they saw the ugly duckling.

"I've never seen anything so ugly," said one.

"What is that?" asked another.

"Come here," called the Old Duck to Mother Duck. "Let me see your children. Hmm! All are very pretty, except that big one."

"He might be ugly," said Mother Duck, "but he swims well."

"Such a pity!" sighed the Old Duck.

Life around the barnyard was very happy for the four yellow ducklings. But the ugly duckling had a terrible time. He was very unhappy. All the ducks and hens teased him because he was so ugly, and no one ever let him join in the fun.

One day, the ugly duckling decided to run away. He scrambled down to the river and began to swim as fast as he could—away from the barnyard, away from Mother Duck, and away from the four beautiful, yellow ducklings. Soon he met two wild geese. "You are ugly," laughed the geese. "You are really so ugly that we cannot help but like you. Won't you come and fly with us?"

But the ugly ducking couldn't leave with them, because he didn't know how to fly.

He walked on and on, until he came to a cottage. Inside the cottage lived an old woman, a cat, and a hen.

"Hiss, hiss!" went the cat.

"Cluck, cluck!" went the hen.

"What, what?" went the old woman. "Looks like we'll be eating duck's eggs from now on."

And so the ugly duckling was allowed to stay. Of course, no eggs appeared. The hen and the cat teased the duckling.

"Can you lay eggs, like me?" asked the hen.

"No," replied the duckling.

"Can you purr, like me?" asked the cat.

"No," replied the duckling.

"Very ugly! Very useless!" said the cat and the hen together.

The ugly duckling wandered back to the river, where he spent his days alone. Soon winter came, and the weather became icy. The duckling grew tired and cold. One day, a farmer rescued the ugly duckling and carried him home. The farmer's children tried to play with him, but, thinking they were teasing him, he jumped into the milk pail. Milk spilled everywhere

"AHHH!"

"Ahhhh!" screamed the farmer's wife.

"Ha! Ha!" laughed the farmer's children.

Luckily the door was open, and the duckling flew out.

The ugly duckling was happy when spring arrived at last. He flapped his wings and soared into the sky. Below, he saw a garden with a large lake in the middle. On the lake were some beautiful white swans.

"I must go down to them," thought the ugly duckling.

He landed on the water and swam toward the swans. They raced forward to meet him. The duckling bent his

head, expecting to be attacked. Instead, he saw his own reflection in the water. He could hardly believe his eyes. He was no longer an ugly gray duckling. He was a beautiful white swan.

As the other swans fussed around their new friend, some children came to the water's edge. "Look, there's a new swan on the lake," cried one. "It's the most beautiful swan I've ever seen." Then the old swans bowed before the young swan. He had never been so happy in his whole life!

Claude, the Lonely Crocodile

Claude the crocodile is lonely. All the other animals in the jungle seem to have lots of brothers and sisters, or lots of friends. They play together all day long, laughing and chasing each other, climbing trees, and running beside the water.

Claude watches them and sighs. No one notices him or asks if he would like to play too. At last, Claude asks his mother if he can have a baby brother to play with.

"Oh, dear, Claude," she says. "I am too busy looking after all my eggs to think about anything else right now. Run along, dear! And please stop looking so miserable! It is a lovely, sunny day. You should be smiling and happy."

"Hey! Watch that tail of yours!" calls his mother. "It almost knocked all my eggs down the bank just now."

Claude sets off for a walk along the riverbank. After a while, he sees Lara Leopard, snoozing in the warm sunshine.

"Lara," says Claude, "do you think one of your little cub brothers will be my baby brother, too?"

"No!" says Lara Leopard. "They are too frightened of your teeth to play with you. And anyway, Mother is washing their ears right now."

Next, Claude calls to Mrs. Parrot, who is chattering in the trees:

"Hello, Mrs. Parrot. You have a lot of babies in your nest. Can you spare one of them to play with me, please?"

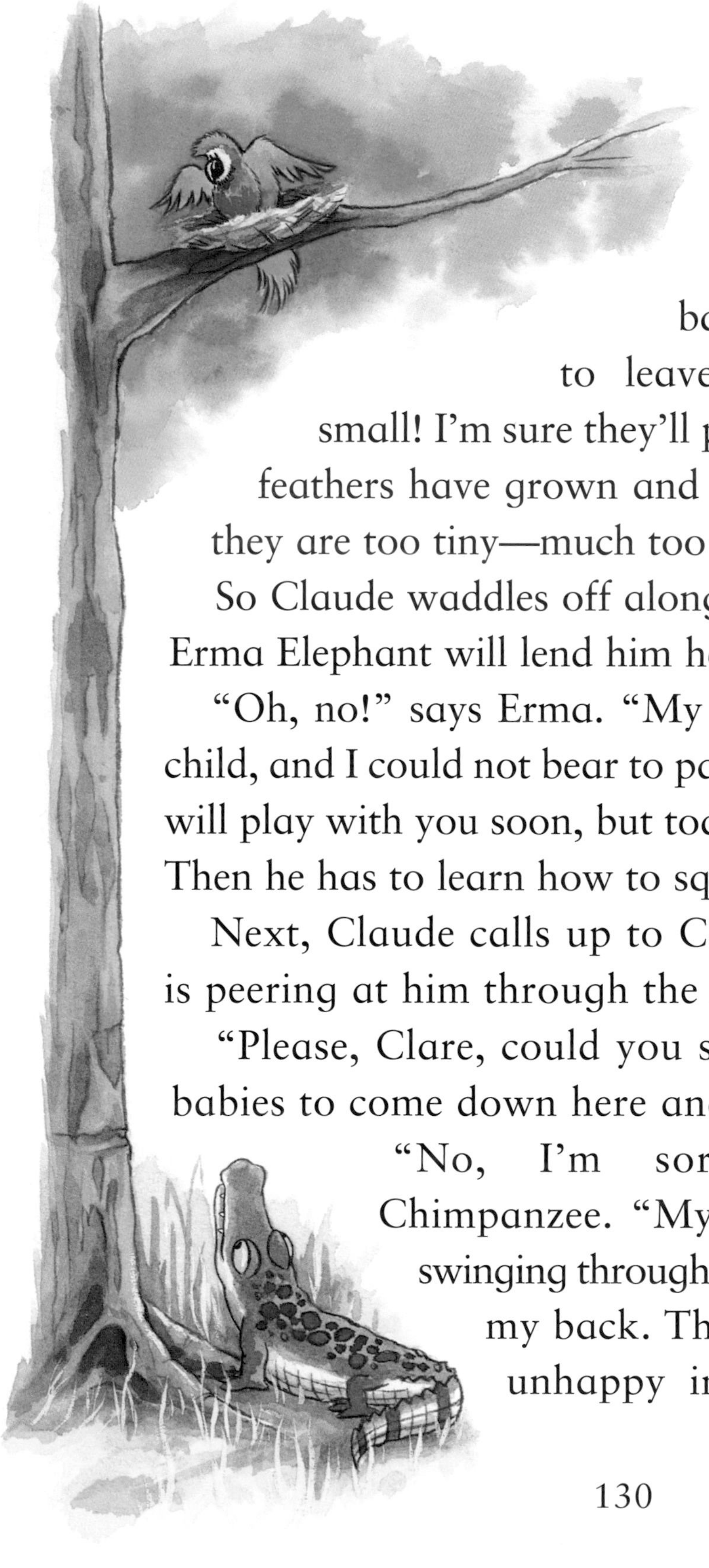

"No, no, no," says Mrs. Parrot. "My little babies are much too small to leave the nest—much too small! I'm sure they'll play with you once their feathers have grown and they can fly. But today they are too tiny—much too tiny!"

So Claude waddles off along the riverbank to see if Erma Elephant will lend him her little son.

"Oh, no!" says Erma. "My darling son is my only child, and I could not bear to part with him. I'm sure he will play with you soon, but today he is having a bath. Then he has to learn how to squirt water."

Next, Claude calls up to Clare Chimpanzee, who is peering at him through the leaves.

"Please, Clare, could you spare one of your twin babies to come down here and play with me?"

"No, I'm sorry," replies Clare Chimpanzee. "My babies like it up here, swinging through the trees and riding on my back. They would be very, very unhappy in your damp swamp.

Sorry, Claude! But don't look so sad. I'm sure that you'll soon find a friend who wants to play."

Claude continues to the edge of the jungle, and then heads out toward the mountains, to the cave where the gorillas live.

"Hello!" he calls. "Hello, little gorillas! Will you please play with me?"

To Claude's surprise, two gorilla babies come running out of the cave. They are very pleased to see him. The cubs start to play with Claude for a while, rolling down the mountainside, laughing and giggling—but then Mother Gorilla calls them back inside.

"Hurry up! It's time for your supper," she says. "Stop playing with Claude and come back into the cave."

"...Supper!"

"Goodbye!" call the two gorilla babies. "Come and play again soon, Claude!"

So now Claude is alone again. He walks slowly back home. He waves to the chimpanzees and the elephants. He waves to the leopards. It is getting late. Bright eyes peep at Claude from the dark shadows as he scurries along the path. At last he reaches the riverbank.

"Quick!" croak the frogs. "Hurry up, Claude! Your mother has a wonderful surprise waiting for you."

Claude rushes up the slippery bank to the top, where his mother is waiting and smiling.

"Look!" grunts his mother proudly. "Look, Claude, my eggs have hatched."

Claude stares in amazement. He cannot believe his eyes. In front of him are ten baby crocodiles. He crouches down to take a closer look. The babies climb up onto Claude and stare at him.

"Hello, Claude," squeak ten little crocodile voices. In an instant the ten little babies are swarming all over Claude, sitting on his head, sliding down his nose, and swinging on his long tail.

"They're tickling me!" he laughs, as his mother watches them carefully—to make sure the little creatures do not fall off Claude's nose or slip down the riverbank.

"You are our very own big brother," squeaks one baby crocodile.

"Will you play with us?" squeaks another.

"Yes! Please! Please play with us!" they all squeak together.

Claude's happy face grins as only a crocodile face can. At last he has brothers and sisters to play with. In fact, he has more brothers and sisters than anyone else in the jungle!

Old MacDonald Had a Farm

Old MacDonald had a farm,
ee-i-ee-i-o!
And on that farm he had some cows,
ee-i-ee-i-o!
With a moo-moo here,
And a moo-moo there,
Here a moo, there a moo, everywhere
a moo-moo,
Old MacDonald had a farm,
ee-i-ee-i-o!

Old MacDonald had a farm,
ee-i-ee-i-o!
And on that farm he had some sheep,
ee-i-ee-i-o!
With a baa-baa here,
And a baa-baa there,
Here a baa, there a baa, everywhere
a baa-baa,
Old MacDonald had a farm,
ee-i-ee-i-o!

Old MacDonald had a farm,
ee-i-ee-i-o!
And on that farm he had some horses,
ee-i-ee-i-o!
With a neigh-neigh here,
And a neigh-neigh there,
Here a neigh, there a neigh, everywhere a
neigh-neigh,
Old MacDonald had a farm,
ee-i-ee-i-o!

Old MacDonald had a farm,
ee-i-ee-i-o!
And on that farm he had some pigs,
ee-i-ee-i-o!
With an oink-oink here,
And an oink-oink there,
Here an oink, there an oink,
everywhere an oink-oink,
Old MacDonald had a farm,
ee-i-ee-i-o!

Old MacDonald had a farm,
ee-i-ee-i-o!
And on that farm he had some ducks,
ee-i-ee-i-o!
With a quack-quack here,
And a quack-quack there,
Here a quack, there a quack,
everywhere a quack-quack,
Old MacDonald had a farm,
ee-i-ee-i-o!

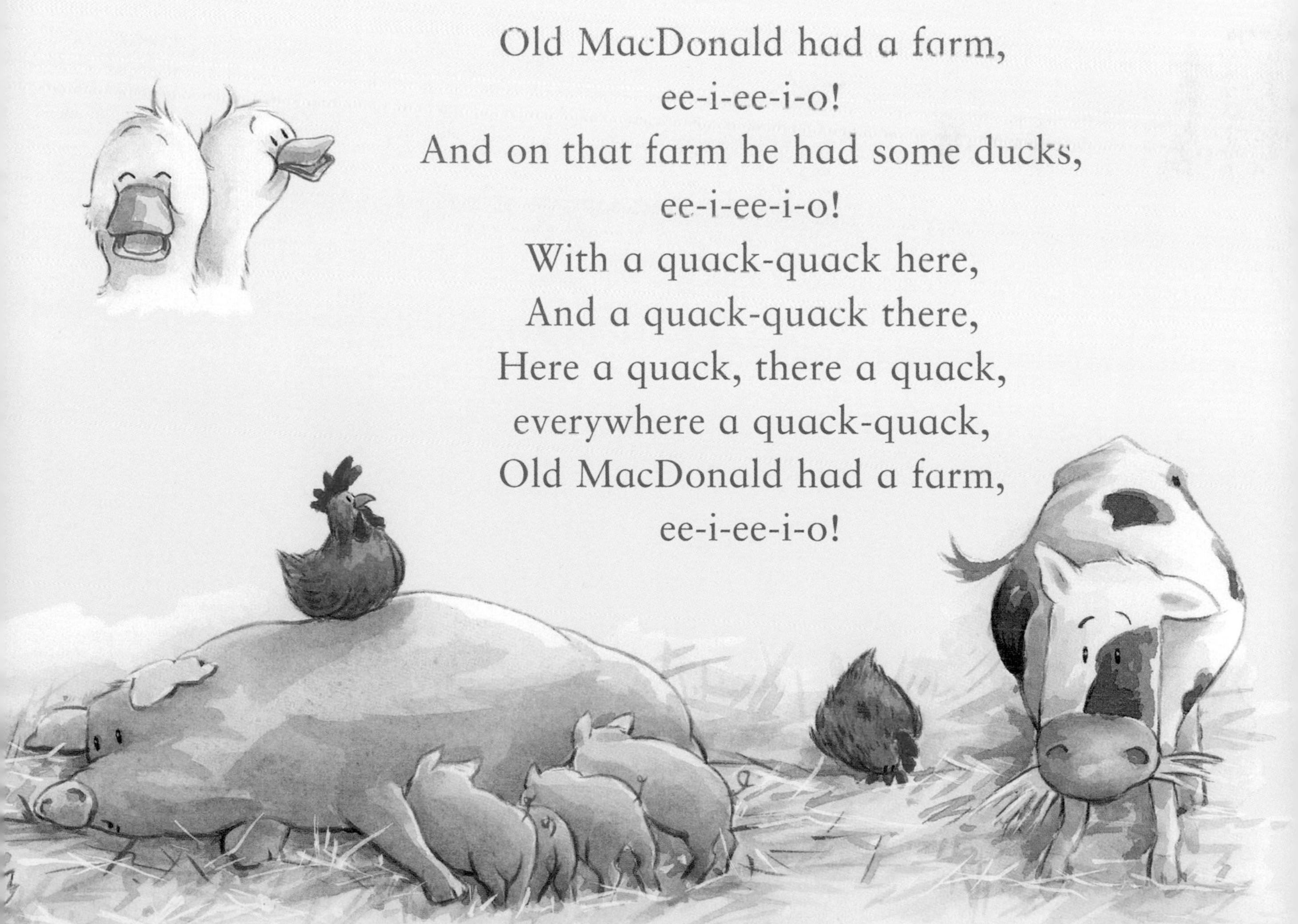

The Princess and the Pea

Once upon a time, in a faraway place, there lived a handsome prince. Now, this prince wanted to get married. But he didn't want to marry an ordinary girl. He wanted to marry a real princess.

The prince traveled from place to place in search of a wife. But the prince didn't know how to tell the difference between a real princess and a pretend one. He found lots of princesses, but there was always something wrong with them. Some were too tall. Some were too small. Some were too silly. Some were too serious. There was even one that was too pretty!

After the prince had traveled far and wide, he began to think he would never, ever find a real princess, and so he returned home. The prince became more and more unhappy. His father and mother, the king and queen, were very worried. They did not know what to do about their sad son.

Then one dark, stormy night there was a knock at

the palace door. The old king himself went to open the door. You can imagine how surprised he was to find a soaking-wet girl shivering before him.

"Come in, come in," said the kind king. "Who are you? Why are you outdoors on such a terrible night?"

"Hello, I'm a princess," the girl told the surprised

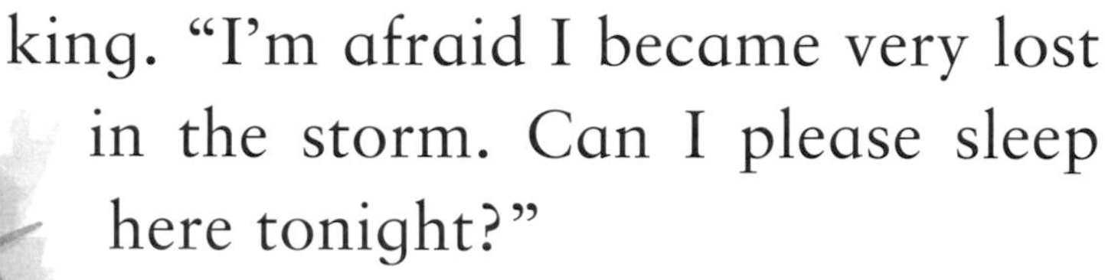

king. "I'm afraid I became very lost in the storm. Can I please sleep here tonight?"

The king stared at the girl in disbelief. But the prince began to smile when he heard her musical voice and saw her beautiful smile. The queen looked carefully at the girl's dripping-wet clothes and wild straggly hair.

"Ah, we shall soon see whether you're a real princess or not," she thought. "There's one sure way of finding out." However, the queen did not tell anyone about her plan.

Quietly, the queen tiptoed into the guest bedroom. She took all the sheets and blankets off the bed and put three tiny peas on top of the mattress. Then she placed twenty more mattresses, one on top of the other, over the peas. Finally, she put twenty

feather quilts on top of the mattresses. The bed was so high that the poor princess needed a ladder to climb onto it.

The next morning, the queen asked the princess how she had slept.

"I hardly slept a wink last night," replied the princess.

"I had a terrible night. There was something very hard in my bed. I'm bruised all over."

Now it was obvious to the queen that only a real princess could feel three tiny peas through twenty mattresses and twenty feather quilts. Everyone agreed that she was indeed a real princess.

The prince was so happy to find a real princess at last, especially such a pretty one. They were married right away and lived a long and happy life together. And as for the three peas—they were put into the royal museum, where you can still see them today. That is, unless they have been stolen by someone who wants to find a real princess!

Sleep, Little Child

Sleep, little child, go to sleep,
Mother is here by thy bed.
Sleep, little child, go to sleep,
Rest on the pillow thy head.

The world is silent and still,
The moon shines bright on the hill,
Then creeps past the windowsill.

Sleep, little child, go to sleep,
Oh, sleep, go to sleep.

The Wheels on the Bus

The wheels on the bus go round and round,
Round and round,
Round and round,
The wheels on the bus go round and round,
All day long.

The horn on the bus goes beep beep beep,
Beep beep beep,
Beep beep beep,
The horn on the bus goes beep beep beep,
All day long.

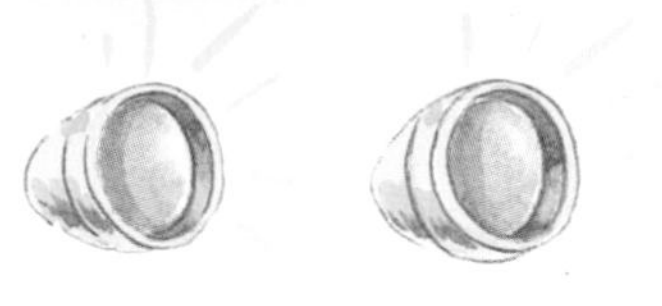
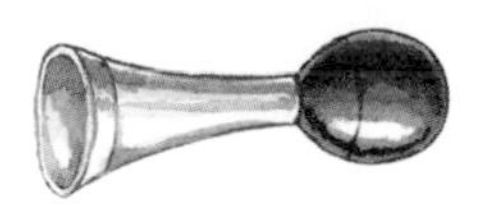

The lights on the bus go blink blink blink,
Blink blink blink,
Blink blink blink,
The lights on the bus go blink blink blink,
All day long.

The doors on the bus, they open and shut,
Open and shut,
Open and shut,
The doors on the bus, they open and shut,
All day long.

The children on the bus go up and down,
Up and down,
Up and down,
The children on the bus go up and down,
All day long.

Thumbelina

Once upon a time, there was a woman who wanted to have a child of her own. The years passed by, and no child came. One day the woman went to see a witch. The witch gave her a stem of barley and told the woman to plant it in a flowerpot.

The woman did as she was told, and a beautiful flower grew. The petals of the flower were shut tight, so the woman kissed them. At once, the petals sprang open, and the woman saw a tiny baby girl inside. The little girl was beautiful, but she was even tinier than the woman's thumb. The woman and her husband decided to call her Thumbelina.

They gave the baby a walnut shell for a bed and a rose leaf for a blanket. She slept in the bed at night and played on the table during the daytime.

Then, one night, an ugly toad jumped onto the table where Thumbelina slept.

"RIBBET!"

"RIBBET!" croaked the toad. "She would make a perfect wife for my son." The toad grabbed Thumbelina as she slept and carried her away to her muddy home.

"RIBBET! RIBBET!" croaked her ugly son,

when he saw the beautiful Thumbelina.

"EEEK," screamed Thumbelina when she saw the two ugly toads. "Ahhh!" she wailed, when the mother toad explained that she wanted Thumbelina to marry her ugly son.

The toads were afraid that Thumbelina might run away. They took her to a lily pad on the river. There was no way that Thumbelina could escape. She cried and she cried. When they heard her sobs, the little fish poked their heads out of the water. Charmed by her beauty, they decided to help the tiny girl. They chewed away at the stem that held the lily pad in place, until at last it was free. Thumbelina floated away.

She floated on and on down the river. Then, one day,

the wind blew so hard that Thumbelina was swept up into the air and carried onto the land.

All through the summer, Thumbelina lived alone in the woods. However, when the winter came she began to feel hungry. She left the wood and made her way into a field. Before too long, she came to a door and knocked on it. When it was opened by a field mouse, Thumbelina begged her for something to eat. Luckily, the field mouse was a kind creature, and she invited Thumbelina into her warm home. The field mouse soon grew to like Thumbelina and invited her to stay.

After Thumbelina had been there for a short time, the field mouse told her about her neighbor, Mr. Mole.

"He's a very rich man. It would be wonderful if you could marry him. Of course, he is blind, so you will have to please him with your pretty voice."

But after meeting Mr. Mole, Thumbelina did not want

to marry him at all. He was indeed rich, but he hated the sunlight and the flowers, even though he had never seen them. Mr. Mole fell in love as soon as he heard Thumbelina's sweet voice. The field mouse and Mr. Mole agreed that he would marry Thumbelina.

Mr. Mole dug a tunnel between their two houses, and one day he gave Thumbelina a guided tour.

Halfway along the tunnel, Mr. Mole kicked aside a dead bird.

"Stupid thing," he grumbled. "It must have died at the beginning of the winter." Thumbelina felt sorry for the bird, but she said nothing.

Later, when the field mouse was asleep, Thumbelina crept back into the tunnel. "Good-bye, dear bird," she whispered. She pressed her head against the bird's chest and, to her surprise, she felt something move. The bird was not dead. It had lain asleep all winter and was now waking up.

For the rest of the winter, Thumbelina nursed the bird, and soon he was well. When spring arrived, Thumbelina smuggled him in through the tunnel and out of the field mouse's door.

"Good-bye," wept Thumbelina, as the bird flew away.

Time passed quickly, and soon Thumbelina's wedding day arrived. Wishing to get one last look at the outside world before entering Mr. Mole's gloomy home, she walked in the field.

"Quiveet, quiveet," came a noise above her head. It was Thumbelina's bird friend. Seeing how unhappy the little girl was, he said, "I'm flying somewhere warm for the winter. Come with me. You can sit on my back."

Thumbelina quickly agreed, and before too long she found herself in a wonderful, warm place. The bird put Thumbelina down on the petals of a beautiful flower. To Thumbelina's surprise, a tiny man with wings was sitting in the center of the flower. He was a flower fairy. At once, he fell in love with the tiny Thumbelina and asked her to marry him. Thumbelina happily agreed.

On their wedding day, Thumbelina received all kinds of presents. The best one of all was a pair of tiny wings. She used them to fly from flower to flower. At last Thumbelina was the happiest girl alive!

Sing a Song of Sixpence

Sing a song of sixpence,
A pocket full of rye;
Four and twenty blackbirds
Baked in a pie.
When the pie was opened,
The birds began to sing;
Wasn't that a dainty dish
To set before the king?

Lavender's Blue

Lavender's blue, dilly, dilly,
Lavender's green;
When I am king, dilly, dilly,
You shall be queen.

Mary Had a Little Lamb

Mary had a little lamb
Its fleece was white as snow;
And everywhere that Mary went
The lamb was sure to go.

It followed her to school one day,
Which was against the rules;
It made the children laugh and play
To see a lamb at school.

Three Blind Mice

Three blind mice, three blind mice.
See how they run, see how they run!
They all ran after the farmer's wife,
Who cut off their tails with a carving knife,
Did you ever hear such a thing in your life,
As three blind mice.

Little Miss Muffet

Little Miss Muffet
Sat on a tuffet,
Eating her curds and whey;
Along came a spider,
Who sat down beside her
And frightened Miss Muffet away.

Rub-a-dub-dub

Rub-a-dub-dub,
Three men in a tub,
And who do you think they be?
The butcher, the baker,
The candlestick-maker,
Turn them out, knaves all three.

Pussycat, Pussycat

Pussycat, pussycat, where have you been?
I've been to London to visit the Queen.
Pussycat, pussycat, what did you do there?
I frightened a little mouse under her chair.

Row, Row, Row Your Boat

Row, row, row your boat
Gently down the stream.
Merrily, merrily, merrily, merrily,
Life is but a dream.

The Fast and Flashy Fish

Swish!

What was that? The warm, blue waters of the Indian Ocean are full of colorful creatures. There are tiny little yellow fish. There are long, thin purple fish.

There are wiggly worms who pretend to be flowers —and flowers who pretend to be wiggly worms. Everything waves and sways in the sea. But,

swish! Somebody is never still. A fast and flashy fish whizzes through the water all day long. He moves so quickly that you can hardly see him. But you can hear him!

Swish! Wish!

"I'm the fastest fish!
No one catches me
In the deep, blue sea!"
That is what the fast and flashy fish sings over and over again.

He wiggles his fins at a starfish. "Let's race, jelly face!" he cries.

"Ready, set, swim!"

"But..." says the starfish. The fast and flashy fish doesn't hear her.

Swish! He is already five rocks away and laughing.

Swish! Wish!

"I'm the fastest fish!
No one catches me
In the deep, blue sea!"

Still, it's not much fun racing an anemone who hardly moves. Under the rocks, the fish sees someone scuttling along.

"Aha!" says the fast and flashy fish. "It's a lobster! Let's have a race, crabby claws! Ready, set, swim!"

"Hey!" says the lobster, lumbering onto the rock. The fast and flashy fish doesn't hear him.

Swish!

He has already reached the other side of an old wreck and is giggling to himself.

Swish! Wish!

"I'm the fastest fish!
No one catches me
In the deep, blue sea!"

The lobster is still complaining, but he's too far away to hear. The fast and flashy fish looks around for someone else to have fun with.

From out of the wreck comes one waving, wiggling leg. Then there are two waving, wiggling legs. Then three, four, five, six, seven . . . eight waving, wiggling legs! It's a large pink octopus!

"Ho! Ho!" says the fast and flashy fish. "This is more like it! Let's have a race, loopy legs! Ready, set, swim!"

"I'm not," says the octopus, angrily, but

the fast and flashy fish is already out in the middle of the coral reef, safe among its beautiful branches.

Swish!
Wish!

"I'm the fastest fish!
No one catches me
In the deep, blue sea!

"It's a pity I can't find someone better to race," grumbles the fast and flashy fish. "This is so boring."

"How about me?" booms a deep, bubbling voice. Overhead, a huge, fat fish is floating. "Come out of the coral," he says, "and we'll see who's the fastest fish."

So the fast and flashy fish

swims up to the big fish. "No problem, flabby fins," he says. "Are you . . . ready, set!"

"Wait!" glugs the big fish. "This isn't fair. We must line up, nose to nose. Come along."

But when the fast and flashy fish lines up beside the fat and floating fish, the bigger fish complains.

"I can't see what you're doing there. I don't mind if you have a little head start. Line your tail up in front of my nose, and then I can see where you are."

The fast and flashy fish laughs and swishes. "No problem, froggy face!" he cries.

"Ready, set..."

"No," says the big fish. "I'll say it. Ready, set. . . gulp!"

The fast and flashy fish has not been seen for a long time in the warm, blue waters of the Indian Ocean. But sometimes, when a huge, fat fish comes floating by, a tiny voice can be heard.

Swish! Wish!

"I'm the *fastest* fish!
In the deep, blue sea!"
How *dark* it can be,

Gulp!

Henny-Penny

It was a quiet day in the country. In the barnyard, Henny-Penny was busy pecking around for grain. "It's very boring here," clucked Henny-Penny. "Nothing exciting ever happens." But just then, PLONK, an acorn fell on her head.

"Goodness gracious!" clucked Henny-Penny. "The sky is falling. I must go and tell the king at once." So away she rushed to tell the king. Before she had gone very far, she bumped into her friend Cocky-Locky.

"Where are you going in such a hurry?" clucked Cocky-Locky.

"The sky is falling," explained Henny-Penny, "and I'm off to tell the king."

"Well, I'm coming with you," said Cocky-Locky, trotting along behind Henny-Penny. Before they had gone much farther, they bumped into their friend Ducky-Lucky.

"Where are you going in such a hurry?" quacked Ducky-Lucky.

"The sky is falling," explained Henny-Penny, "and we're off to tell the king."

"Well, I'm coming with you," said Ducky-Lucky, waddling along behind Henny-Penny and Cocky-Locky. They hadn't gone far when they met their friend Goosey-Loosey.

"Where are you going in such a hurry?" honked Goosey-Loosey.

"The sky is falling," explained Henny-Penny, "and we're off to tell the king."

"Well, I'm coming with you," said Goosey-Loosey, swaying along behind Henny-Penny, Cocky-Locky, and Ducky-Lucky. What a strange sight they made!

Next, they met Foxy-Loxy. None of them knew her very well.

"Where are you going in such a hurry?" asked Foxy-Loxy.

"The sky is falling," said Henny-Penny, "and we're off to tell the king."

"Ah," smiled Foxy-Loxy. "You're going the wrong way. Follow me, I'll show you the way."

"What a nice fox!" clucked Henny-Penny, as she and her three friends followed Foxy-Loxy. On and on they followed her until they reached a cave.

"This is a shortcut," said Foxy-Loxy. "Don't be afraid, and stay close to me."

The unlucky birds didn't know it, but this wasn't really a shortcut —it was Foxy-Loxy's den.

Next, Goosey-Loosey, Ducky-Lucky, and Cocky-Locky quickly followed Foxy-Loxy into the cave.

Henny-Penny was about to join them when

COCK-A-DOODLE-DOO!

Cocky-Locky let out a terrible scream.

Henny-Penny ran as fast as she could until she reached the safety of the barnyard. Meanwhile, Foxy-Loxy made a fine feast out of Cocky-Locky, Ducky-Lucky, and Goosey-Loosey.

Henny-Penny never did get to tell the king that the sky was falling. But, then again, the sky never was falling, was it? Wasn't Henny-Penny a silly hen?

The Wolf and the Raccoon

The wind howled and the wind moaned. The wolf tucked her big brush tail around her face even more tightly, sheltering her delicate eyes and delicate nose-tip from the cruel winter. Inside her thick fur were tiny, warm pockets of air that protected her from the cold, just like a quilt.

Wolf slept, and as she slept, the snow fell heavy from the dull white snow clouds and landed along the green branches that crisscrossed above.

A small furry ball of a creature came scampering across the hard, woody branches, skimming the prickly needles. Along she came, hopping and skipping, tripping lightly on delicate feet. She was a raccoon,

ears pert, looking for entertainment.

Raccoon spotted Wolf and stopped. She tipped her head this way and that, wondering about a trick, and before she knew it she had turned a quick somersault, landed back on the snow-laden branch—and catapulted a big clump of snow onto the wolf's head.

"Eer! Eer!"

Wolf jumped up with a start. She cowered low, darting her eyes this way and that to find her attacker. But she could see nothing, and retreated to the shelter of a thick tree trunk, her eyes sharp, looking every way—except up.

THWACK!

Another clump of snow landed squarely on her head. This time she looked up. There was the daring raccoon with her ringed tail, dark-furred eyes, and soft black nose.

"Grrrah!" roared the wolf.

"Grrrah!" mimicked the raccoon, feeling safe up the tree.

But wolves can climb too if they have to, and this wolf had to! She aimed for the lowest branch with her thick-clawed

paws, and dragged herself up to a place just underneath Raccoon.

But the raccoon was still smiling. And before jumping higher onto the next branch, she brushed her ringed tail delicately over a snow clump, sending a shower of speckles down onto the wolf's face.

"Shrrrrrrrr!" screeched Wolf, who was so angry that she leaped even higher up the tree.

And so the two furry creatures jumped up and across and down and along, moving through the great fir trees with such speed that they thoroughly annoyed all the other creatures of the forest.

"Oouch!" complained the snowy owls, as they were flicked in their beaks by a twanging branch.

"Brrrrrr!" complained the deer, huddled up close, trying to get comfortable against the cold.

"Cooeeeee!" called the playful beavers, who wanted

to join in. But their father held them back, saying that this was a grown-up game.

"SHFFFFRRRRR!" roared Wolf ferociously.

"Eer! Eer!" mocked Raccoon from high in a tree.

But soon the two creatures stood panting. Raccoon was clamped safely onto a branch with her tail twisted around it, and Wolf was perched on a branch too thin for her weight. The branch was bending more and more by the moment, until,

"SPROING!"

—it sprang back and catapulted Wolf in a high arc through the air, up to the place where Raccoon was gathering her breath.

"EEEEEEEK!" both creatures cried together as

they collided and fell headlong down the height of the giant fir tree and far to the ground.

But they didn't hurt themselves. Instead, the wolf and the raccoon landed in a heap on a white-padded blanket of snow. They looked at one another in silence, while all around the wind moaned and the wind howled. The swirling cold of the wintry forest crept slowly, slowly through the warm pockets of fur on their backs, even reaching their skin.

Their eyes stung. Their noses turned blue. And Wolf and Raccoon started to giggle.

"Shall we save our energy?" suggested the wolf.

"Oh, yes indeed," said the raccoon.

The two furry creatures intertwined tails in an instant, tucked their delicate eyes and pointed noses deep down into their shared fur, and slept through another night of winter, until morning, when at last spring began.

Tom Thumb

Late one night, a poor farmer and his wife sat talking in their kitchen. "It is a shame we have no children," said the farmer.

"Oh, yes, dear," agreed his wife. "I'd be happy if we had just one child. I'd love that child even if it was no bigger than my thumb."

Not long after that, the wife's wish was granted. She gave birth to a baby boy. He was strong and healthy, but he was no bigger than her thumb. The couple were delighted and called their new baby Tom Thumb.

The years passed, but tiny Tom stayed the same size as the day he was born. Although he was very small, Tom was smart and helpful.

One day, the farmer was getting ready to go into the forest to cut wood. "If only I had someone to bring the cart along later," he sighed.

"I'll bring it," said Tom Thumb.

"Tom," laughed his father, "you're much too small!"

"Don't worry," said Tom Thumb. "Just get Mother to harness the horse and I'll do the rest."

Later, after his mother had harnessed the horse, Tom asked her to put him inside the horse's ear. From there, Tom told the horse where to go. All went well, and soon Tom and the cart had reached the woods. Then, as Tom was shouting "Steady! Steady!" two strangers walked past.

"That's funny!" said one. "I can hear someone directing that cart. Yet nobody is there. Let's see where it goes."

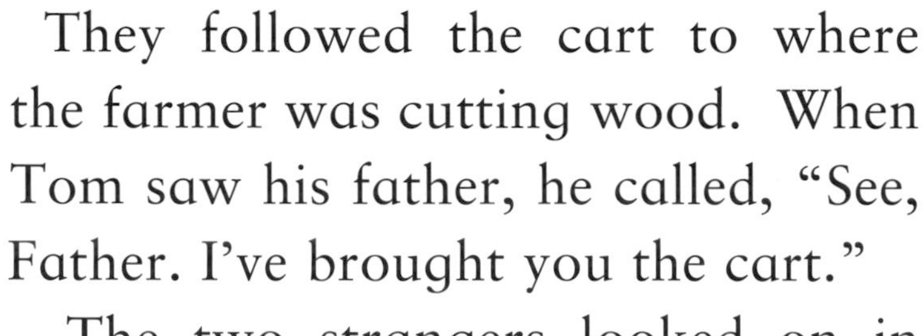

They followed the cart to where the farmer was cutting wood. When Tom saw his father, he called, "See, Father. I've brought you the cart."

The two strangers looked on in astonishment as Tom's father pulled Tom out of the horse's ear. "That little chap could make us our fortune," whispered one of the strangers. "We could take him from town to town, and people would pay us to see him."

So the two strangers went up to the farmer and asked, "How much do you want for the little man?"

"I wouldn't sell him for all the gold in the world," replied the farmer.

However, on hearing the strangers' words, Tom had an idea. He climbed onto his father's shoulder and whispered into his ear, "Take their money. I'll soon come back." So the farmer gave Tom to the two strangers, and received a large bag of gold coins in return.

After saying goodbye to his father, Tom was carried off by

the strangers.

They walked for a while until Tom said, “Put me down!” When the man did as Tom asked, the tiny boy ran off and hid in a mouse hole.

“Goodbye!” shouted Tom. “You should have kept a closer eye on me.”

The two men searched for Tom, but it was no use. At last they gave up and went home without him. Tom crept out of the mouse hole and walked along the path until he found a barn, where he went to sleep in the hay.

The next morning, the milkmaid got up to feed the cows. She went to the barn and grabbed an armful of hay—the same hay in which Tom was sleeping. Poor Tom knew nothing about it, until he found himself inside the stomach of one of the cows.

It was a dark place, and more and more hay kept coming into the cow’s stomach. The space left for Tom grew smaller and smaller. At last, Tom

cried, "No more hay!"

The milkmaid ran to the dairy farmer in fright. "Sir, the cow is talking," she cried.

"Are you mad?" asked the farmer, but he went to the barn to see for himself.

"No more hay!" shouted Tom. This bewildered the farmer, who sent for the vet.

The vet operated on the cow, and out popped a bunch of hay. Tom was hidden inside it. The hay was thrown onto the manure heap. Just as Tom was preparing to escape, a hungry wolf ran by and gulped down Tom and the hay.

Refusing to give up hope, Tom said to the wolf, "I know where you can get a mighty feast."

"Where?" asked the wolf.

Quickly, Tom described the way to his father's house.

That night, the wolf climbed in through the farmer's kitchen window. Once inside, he ate so much food and grew so fat that he couldn't squeeze back out of the window. This was just what Tom had planned. He began to jump around in the wolf's stomach and shout as loud as he could.

Very soon, the farmer and his wife were awoken by the noise. They rushed into the kitchen.

Seeing the wolf, the farmer grabbed his ax and aimed it at the animal. Suddenly he heard Tom's voice shouting, "Father, I am inside the wolf's stomach."

Overjoyed, the farmer killed the wolf with a single blow to his head. Then he cut Tom out of its stomach.

From that day on, Tom

stayed at home with his parents. Now he knew for sure that there is no place like home!

Ug-Ug-Ugly

Long, long, long ago, a huge egg lay in a nest. The egg wobbled, then wobbled a bit more. It rolled a bit, then rolled a bit more. It rolled right over the edge of the nest—WOOOOOOOOO!

Bump! Crack! Plick! Out popped a wrinkly, goggle-eyed, ugly-faced baby dinosaur. He squinted at the wide world all around. Everything looked scary. Through the leaves peeked

one,

two,

three,

four

wrinkly, goggle-eyed, ugly-faced toddler dinosaurs. They stared at the new baby as he began to wriggle out of his eggshell.

"Ug!" said the first toddler.

"Ug!" said the second.

"Ug!" said the third.

"Ug!" said the fourth, nodding her head. "You're UGLY!"

The baby dinosaur stood up on his thin new legs and crept away into the shadow of a dark, drooping flower.

The toddler dinosaurs skipped off happily, calling:

"So long, now!"

"Little monster!"

"Come and find us!"

"See you soon!"

Then through the trees burst a wrinkly, goggle-eyed, ugly-faced mommy dinosaur.

"La-di-da!" sang Mommy. "My egg should be hatched by now—la-di-da!"

But when she peered into her nest,

"Huh?" said Mommy. "Where's my baby?"

And **thump! thump! thump!** she trudged off through the steamy forest to look for him. She thumped around the bursting volcano, across the gushing river, and through the gurgling swamp, but

she couldn't find her baby anywhere.

So Mommy sat down and frowned, and forced her pea-sized brain to think. And think it did. It thought about an egg. It thought about an eggshell.

"EGGSHELL!" she exclaimed, as she thump, thump, thumped back through the gurgling swamp, across the gushing river, around the bursting volcano, and through the steamy forest to the place where she had built her nest.

This time she didn't look inside the nest, but on the ground below it.

"Eggshell!" she whispered, when she spotted a fleck of shiny green shell.

"Eggshell!" she announced, when she spotted more flecks of shell farther along.

"Huh?" said Mommy when the trail of eggshell stopped.

She sat down and frowned, and forced her pea-sized brain to think. And think it did. It thought about a baby.

"WHERE'S MY BABY?" called Mommy at the top of her voice.

"Here we are!" replied her four wrinkly, goggle-eyed, ugly-faced toddler dinosaurs.

"You're not babies!" she said. "I'm talking about the baby who came out of that eggshell. He must be here somewhere."

The toddlers all silently pointed toward the same place.

Mommy dinosaur

gently lifted the head of a drooping flower and there, curled up in a ball, was her baby.

"Ug!" said the first toddler.

"Ug!" began the second, before Mommy interrupted.

"My baby!" Mommy cried, as she gathered the dinosaur in her huge claws. She looked around proudly at her ugly children. "Isn't he lovely?" admired Mommy. "What should we call him?"

"Ugly?" suggested one of the toddlers.

"Don't be so unkind!" scolded Mommy, stroking her newly hatched baby. "Poor little thing—imagine thinking of that!"

"Eggshell?" suggested another, as the baby gurgled loudly.

"He likes that name!" all the toddler dinosaurs called out together.

Mommy sat down and frowned, and forced her pea-sized brain to think. And think it did. It thought about a perfect name for her baby

dinosaur. It thought of the long journey Mommy had made to find him.

And the name she came up with was . . .

"GURGLING SWAMP!"

She called out the name at the top of her voice, as the baby gave a huge burp.

"Yay!" cheered the toddlers, who thought this was a very good name for the wrinkly, goggle-eyed, ugly-faced baby dinosaur who was happily burping (or gurgling) in his mommy's arms.

Star Light, Star Bright

Star light, star bright,
First star I see tonight,
I wish I may, I wish I might,
Have the wish I wish tonight.

It's Raining, It's Pouring

It's raining, it's pouring,
The old man is snoring;
He went to bed and bumped his head
And couldn't get up in the morning!

Hickory, Dickory, Dock

Hickory, dickory, dock. The mouse ran up the clock.
The clock struck one, the mouse ran down,
Hickory, dickory, dock.

I Had a Little Nut Tree

I had a little nut tree
And nothing would it bear
But a silver nutmeg
And a golden pear.

The King of Spain's daughter
Came to visit me,
And all for the sake
Of my little nut tree.

Simple Simon

Simple Simon met a pieman
Going to the fair;
Said Simple Simon to the pieman,
"Let me taste your ware."

Mrs. Hen

Chook, chook, chook, chook, chook,
Good morning, Mrs. Hen.
How many chickens have you got?
Madam, I've got ten.
Four of them are yellow,
And four of them are brown,
And two of them are speckled red,
The nicest in the town.

Ride a Cock Horse

Ride a cock horse to Banbury Cross
To see a fine lady upon a white horse.
Rings on her fingers and bells on her toes,
She shall have music wherever she goes.

The Frog Prince

Once upon a time there lived a young princess. She had lots and lots of toys, but her favorite one was a golden ball. She carried it with her wherever she went.

One day the princess set off for a walk in the woods. When she grew tired, she sat down beside a pool to rest. As she sat there, she threw her golden ball into the air and caught it. Higher and higher she threw the ball, until one time it soared so high that she couldn't catch it. SPLASH! The ball fell into the pool. The princess peered into the dark water, but it was so deep that she couldn't see the bottom.

"Oh, no!" wailed the princess. "My ball is lost. I

would give anything—even my fine clothes and jewels—anything, just to have my ball back."

Just then she heard a noise:

"RIBBET! RIBBET!"

A frog popped its ugly head out of the water and said, "Dear Princess, what is wrong? Why are you crying?"

"Eeeek!" screamed the princess. She was not used to meeting frogs that could talk. "Wh . . . what can a nasty frog do to help me? My golden ball has fallen into the pool. Now it is gone forever!"

"Don't cry," croaked the frog. "If you will just let me eat from your plate and sleep on your pillow, I will find your ball."

"Hmm!" thought the princess. "This slimy frog will never be able to get out of the water. If it finds my ball, I won't have to do any of those silly things." So she turned to the frog and lied, "If you bring back my ball, I promise to do everything you ask."

At that, the frog ducked beneath the water. In no time at all, he was back with the ball in his mouth. He threw it at the princess's feet. Delighted, the princess snatched the ball and ran home as fast as she could. Not once did she think to say thank you to the frog. Indeed, she forgot all about him.

"Wait for me!" croaked the frog. But the princess was gone.

The next evening, as the princess sat down to dinner, she heard a strange noise:

PLISH, PLASH, PLISH!

It sounded as if something wet was coming up the stairs. Then there was a TAP, TAP on the door and a little voice croaked,

"Open the door, my one true love.
Open the door, my turtle dove.
Remember the promise you made in the wood?
Well, now is the time to make it come good."

The princess opened the door, and there stood the frog. Frightened, she slammed the door in his face.

"What's the matter?" asked her father, the king.

The princess told him all about her lost ball and her promise to the frog.

"You must always keep a promise, my dear," the king said to his daughter. "Go and let him in." So the princess opened the door.

The frog hopped in and made his way to the table.

–PLISH, PLASH, PLISH!–

"Lift me up to sit beside you," said the frog. Wrinkling her nose, the princess did as he asked.

"Push your plate closer so that I can eat from it," said the frog. Closing her eyes, the princess did as he asked. When the frog had eaten as much as he could, he croaked, "I'm tired. Carry me upstairs and let me sleep in your bed." With a large frown on her face, the princess did as he asked.

Within minutes, the frog was snoring away on the princess's pillow.

And there he slept until it was morning. Then he awoke and hopped away without so much as a

RIBBET. "Hooray!" cried the princess. "That should be the last I see of that silly old creature."

But the princess was wrong. That evening, the frog knocked on the door once more, and croaked,

"Open the door, my one true love.
Open the door, my turtle dove.
Remember the promise you made in the wood?
Well, now is the time to make it come good."

The princess opened the door and

PLISH, PLASH, PLISH!

—in hopped the frog.

Once again, he ate from the princess's plate and slept on her pillow until morning.

By the third evening, the princess was beginning to like the frog a little. "His eyes are quite lovely," she thought, as she drifted off to sleep.

But when the princess awoke the next morning, she

was astonished to find a handsome prince standing beside her bed. The frog was nowhere to be seen. As she gazed into the prince's strangely familiar eyes, he explained how an evil fairy had cast a spell on him and turned him into an ugly frog. The spell could only be broken when a princess let him eat from her plate and sleep in her bed for three nights.

"Now you have broken the spell, and I wish to ask for your hand in marriage," said the prince.

Being a princess, she quickly agreed, and before the prince could say "RIBBET," a fine coach and a handsome horse appeared. Together they rode off to the prince's home, where they lived happily ever after.

Runaway Ragtime

Ragtime was a large black-and-white cat who lived in a busy town. He loved his town, with its winding side streets, its busy supermarkets, and its yummy trashcans.

So when Ragtime's family, the Pips, moved to the country, Ragtime wasn't at all happy. He didn't like it one little bit. He didn't like the trees. He didn't like the fields. He didn't like the streams.

One morning, Ragtime was feeling very bored. Mrs. Pip had gone to work, and Mr. Pip was taking Thomas and Tillie to school. Ragtime decided to climb over the backyard fence into the field beyond. He was running away to have an

adventure.

Ragtime hadn't gone far when he bumped into a blackbird, who was juggling pebbles on its beak. "Hello!" said Ragtime. "I'm Runaway Ragtime. I'm having an adventure."

"Hello!" squawked the blackbird. "I'm Beaker. Can I come too?"

"Of course!" replied Ragtime, and the two new friends set off together. Soon Ragtime and Beaker reached a babbling stream. Suddenly a frog appeared out of the reeds, doing cartwheels.

"Hello!" said Ragtime. "I'm Runaway Ragtime. I'm having an adventure."

"And I'm Beaker," squawked Beaker. "I juggle pebbles on my beak."

"Hello!" gulped the frog. "I'm Monica. I can do cartwheels. Can I come too?"

"Of course!" replied Ragtime, and the three friends set off together.

As they crossed a plank over the stream, they discovered a duck whistling a tune.

"Hello!" said Ragtime. "I'm Runaway Ragtime. I'm having an adventure."

"Hello!" squawked the blackbird. "I'm Beaker. I juggle pebbles on my beak."

"Hello!" said Monica. "I'm Monica, the cartwheeling frog."

"Good job!" quacked the duck. "I'm Ronda. I whistle tunes. Can I come too?"

And so the four friends set off together toward the woods, where they chanced upon a dancing mouse and a smiling snail.

"Hello!" said Ragtime. "I'm Runaway Ragtime. I'm having an adventure."

"Yes!" squawked Beaker. "I'm Beaker, and I juggle pebbles on my beak."

"Hello!" said Monica. "I'm Monica, and I do cartwheels."

"That's true," quacked Ronda. "I'm Ronda. Listen to me whistle."

"That's good," squeaked the mouse. "I'm Didgeri,

and this is Angelo. He's a very talented snail. We like adventures. Can we come too?"

"Of course!" replied Ragtime, and all the friends set off together. They made their way through some tall trees and came to a farm. In the meadow beside the farmhouse stood a very large bull.

"Hello!" said Ragtime. "I'm Runaway Ragtime, and these are my new friends. We're all having an adventure."

"Yes!" squawked Beaker."I'm Beaker. I juggle pebbles on my beak."

"Hello!" said Monica. "I'm Monica. I do cartwheels."

"That's true," quacked Ronda. "I'm Ronda. I whistle tunes."

"Hello!" squeaked Didgeri. "I'm Didgeri, and I dance. And this is Angelo, a very talented snail."

"Oh, that's nice. Lovely. So you're all having an adventure," snorted the bull. "I'm Barney McCabe."

Barney's horns glistened in the afternoon sun.

"Now run for your lives!"

Runaway Ragtime swung around as Beaker flew up into the air, showering pebbles everywhere. One of the pebbles whizzed past Monica as she was cartwheeling away. On and on it whizzed, past whistling Ronda and dancing Didgeri, with the very talented Angelo sliding along as fast as he could.

What a chase it was! Snort! Meow! Squawk! Gulp! Quack! Whistle! Squeak! Hah! Pah! Boing! Snort! WHAT A CHASE!

Boing! Snort! WHAT A CHASE!

And all the time Barney McCabe was catching up, catching up . . . CATCHING UP with the talented band as across the meadow, through the woods, over the stream, and into the field they ran. HELP!

As they raced into the field Ragtime recognized something familiar—HOME! The home that was so boring he'd run away from it, but oh, how happy he was to see it now!

First Ragtime, and then all his friends, dashed, flew, cartwheeled, bounced, danced, and hopped over the fence. Barney McCabe stopped, snorted, and, with a big

grin, headed slowly back toward his farm.

The back door of Ragtime's house opened. Mr. and Mrs. Pip, Thomas, and Tillie gasped in amazement when right in front of them they saw a juggling blackbird, a cartwheeling frog, a whistling duck, a dancing mouse, a very talented snail named Angelo, and . . . one very happy cat, Runaway Ragtime. He had returned home. And he wasn't planning to have any more adventures . . . well, not for a while, anyway.

The Three Little Pigs and the Wolf

Snort!

Early one morning
The sun came out,
And out set three pigs
Snorting their snouts.
SNORT!

Snort!

The three little pigs—Oink, Grunt, and Curly—walked up the hills and down the dales until their cheeks were quite pink.

TEE-HEE!

They walked to the woods
Where the path split in three,
And the three little pigs said:
"TEE-HEE!"

TEE-HEE!

The pigs set off in different directions. Oink went this way, Grunt went that way, and Curly went . . . well . . .

Curly felt sad
As she trotted alone,
But then found some straw
For building her home.
HOME!

When her house was finished, Curly gathered some extra straw to make a table and chair for the inside. And, last of all, she braided a little straw bed so that she would have a cozy night's sleep. But . . .

Along came a wolf
With a scary big frown,
Sharp teeth and a huff,
And a blow your house down.
DOWN!

Poor Curly. Her straw house was no more. How she ran and ran, up the hills and down the valley, to escape from that horrible wolf.

Meanwhile,

Grunt snapped some sticks
From branches of wood
To make a new home
In the best way she could.
HOME!

When her house was finished, Grunt gathered some extra sticks to make a table and chair for the inside. And, last of all, she wove a little stick bed so that she would have a cozy night's sleep. But . . .

Along came the wolf
With a scary big frown,
Sharp teeth and a huff,
And a blow your house down.
DOWN!

Poor Grunt. Her stick house was no more. How she ran and ran, up the hills and down the dales, to escape from that horrible wolf.

Meanwhile,

Oink was struggling
With big heavy bricks,
But a brick house was stronger
Than a house made of sticks.
STICKS? POOH!

When her house was finished, Oink gathered some extra bricks to make a table and chair for the inside. And, last of all, she stacked some bricks for a little brick bed so that she would have a . . . well . . . probably extremely uncomfortable night's sleep.

Meanwhile . . . Curly and Grunt were still running, up hills and down dales, until their cheeks were quite pink. They were running to the place where their sister had built her house made of bricks.

Curly and Grunt ran,
Ran all the way,
Away from the wolf
To Oink's house to stay.
HOORAY! HOORAY!
HOORAY!

When, of course . . .

Along came the wolf
With a scary big frown,
Sharp teeth and a huff,
And a blow your house down.
DOWN! NOT DOWN!

Inside the brick house,
Oink, Grunt, and Curly felt very safe.

Outside the brick house, the wolf's cheeks were growing redder and redder and hotter and hotter from all that huffing and puffing.

The brick house stayed up,
The wolf tumbled down,
Down a steep hill,
Still wearing his frown.
SNORT! SWEET! SNORT!

When the wolf was gone, Grunt wove some sticks in a clever way to make three little chairs. Oink made two more brick beds—one for each of her sisters.

And Curly used her straw-braiding skills to make a lovely soft mattress to put on top of the brick beds. And the three little pigs had a very cozy night's sleep.

Good night!

Polly Penguin Wants to Fly

Penguins are wonderful swimmers. They can dive down deep. They can twist and roll in the water. They can swim as fast as any fish. But no penguin has ever learned to fly.

"It's not fair!" says Polly Penguin, watching the gulls wheeling in the bright blue sky above her head. "I want to fly, too. Like all the other birds."

"I want to fly," says Polly to her mother, as they waddle out to join their friends on the big, steep ice slide.

"Don't be silly," says her mother. "This is much more fun!"

And then they both slide down on their tummies, all the way into the ocean.

"This is lots of fun," agrees Polly, as they scramble out of the water. "But I still want to fly."

"Have you ever learned to fly?" Polly asks Wise Old Whale as he cruises along beside her.

Wheeeeeee!

"Not really," says Whale. "But every now and then I leap out of the water and fly through the air, just for a moment or two."

"I will try that," says Polly, jumping out of the sea and sailing high into the air before landing on the ice again.

"That was lots of fun!" laughs Polly, as she runs across an iceberg with hundreds of other penguins and jumps into the ocean.

Wheeeeeee!

"And so is this, but I still want to fly, too."

She lands with a big splash right next to Snowy, the white seal.

"Hello, Polly!" says Snowy.

"Hello, Snowy!" says Polly. "Have you ever learned to fly?"

"Not really," replies Snowy. "But every now and then I take a deep breath, stretch out my flippers, flick my tail, and shoot through the water so fast that it feels as if I am flying, just for a moment or two."

"I will try that," says Polly, flashing so fast through the waves that, just for a moment, she really does seem to be flying.

Wheeeeeee!

"Can you fly?" Polly asks Fluffy Rabbit as she scampers over the snow.

"Not really," says Fluffy Rabbit. "But sometimes I jump so high that I think I might take off into the sky. It is good to skip and hop just for fun sometimes. Will you join me?"

So Polly skips and jumps and hops and rolls in the snow with Fluffy until it is dark.

The air is turning icy cold and the stars are coming out as Polly sets off for home. On the way she meets Reindeer, who is busy polishing his antlers in the snow.

"My mom says you are only here for a flying visit," says Polly. "So can you fly? Where are your wings?"

"No, little Polly, I am afraid that I cannot fly," answers Reindeer sadly. "Although there are stories about some lucky reindeer who can."

He stares up into the night sky.

"But now," he says, "it is getting very late. I think you should be at home, Polly. Your mom will be worried."

"Yes," says Polly, "I must hurry." And she scampers off, sliding over the ice.

"Wait!" calls Reindeer. "I can give you a ride." So Polly hops up onto Reindeer's back, and she hangs on tightly to his antlers as he gallops all the way home.

"This is wonderful!" cries Polly.

The air rushes past her, and they seem to fly through the night.

Wheeeeeee!

"Thank you," says Polly to Reindeer, sliding off his back by her front door. "That really did feel like flying. It was great. Can I have a ride again tomorrow?"

Reindeer nods. He is happy to have a new friend.

"Well, did you learn to fly today?" asks Dad, as Polly scuttles inside.

"Not exactly, not really. But . . . well, yes, in a way,"

replies Polly, smiling.

"Well, what a funny mixed-up answer!" laughs her father.

"Oh, I went so fast that it felt like flying," explains Polly. "And I was high up in the air—and it was just like magic."

"Good!" says Polly's mom. "Now it is time for supper. I have been flying around everywhere, too—sliding and shopping and cooking. And your father has been jumping off icebergs and racing and fishing, so we have all had an exciting, busy day. Now let's enjoy our fish supper together."

And they do.

As Polly eats her delicious fish, she dreams of riding on Reindeer's back again. One day, maybe, if she is really lucky, she will meet those special reindeer who can really fly—and soar right up into the midnight sky. Wouldn't that be exciting?

The Naughty Little Rabbits

Three little rabbits lived with their mama in a cozy burrow on a hillside. When they were hungry, Mama took them upstairs to nibble on the meadow grass. She showed them games, like Bunny Hop and Rolling-Down-the-Hill. At night, she tucked them safely into their sleeping corners, down in the deep, dim burrow.

Each little rabbit had its own cozy sleeping corner, which had been dug out of the side of the burrow. It was very snug. The rabbits liked to nestle in their corners and listen to their mama while she worked at night. She would sweep out the burrow and make everything tidy, murmuring a soft little rabbit lullaby.

But one day, Mama said, "Oh, my! You're getting bigger and taller every day! Soon you won't fit into your corners. We need to scrape and scrabble, and make them bigger. Come and help me!"

"No, no, no!" cried the little rabbits. "Come upstairs in the sunshine and play with us!"

"First there is work to do," their mama said. "If you help me, I can come with you. I will show you lots of lovely games. I will find delicious things for us to eat. But first I need you to help me do this work!"

But the naughty little rabbits wouldn't listen. "No! No! No!" they cried. And off they ran, upstairs and out of the burrow.

They had never been outside before without their mama. Now here they were, out in the big bright meadow, with nothing to do and nobody to play with.

"I don't know what to

do," said the first little rabbit. "I wish we had someone to play with."

Just then, a squirrel ran out of the woods at the edge of the meadow.

"Come and play with me," cried the squirrel. "I know lots of games. Just come along with me, and do what I do."

So they did.

The squirrel ran and jumped right over a stone. So did the little rabbit children.

The squirrel ran and jumped off the end of a log. So did the little rabbit children.

The squirrel ran, and zipped right up a tree.

"Oh, no!" cried the little rabbits.

"Yah, yah! Got you!" cried the squirrel. He laughed and jeered at the little rabbits down below. Then he began to throw hard little acorns on top of their heads.

"Ow, ow, ow!" cried the little rabbits. They all ran away, as fast they could go.

When the little rabbits stopped, they were at the bottom of the hill, next to a river.

"Oh, I'm hungry," said the second little rabbit. "I wish we had something to eat."

Just then, a frog popped out of the river. "Come and have lunch with me," said the frog. "I have lots of things to eat. Just do what I do."

The little rabbit children gathered around.

"Sit very still," said the frog. So they did.

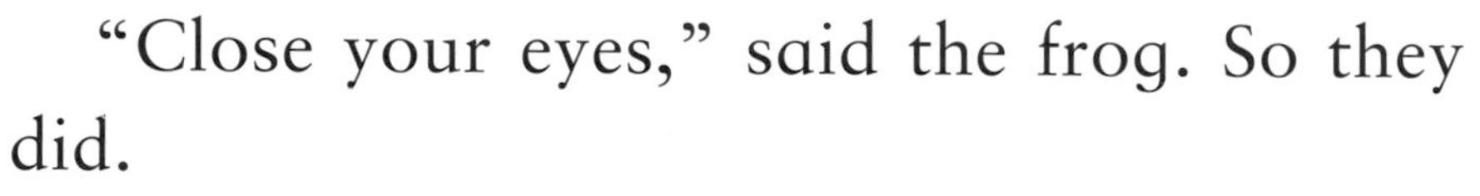

"Close your eyes," said the frog. So they did.

"Stick out your tongues," said the frog.

"YUM!" said the frog, as he swallowed a big, fat fly.

"Yuck! Yuck! Yuck!" cried the rabbits.

They coughed and spat until they were all worn out.

"I'm so tired," said the third little rabbit. "I wish we could take a cozy nap."

A cloud came over the sun and it grew dark. It turned cold. Rain started to fall.

Plop! Plop! Plop! came the raindrops.

"Help! Oh, help!" cried the little rabbits.

Just then, they heard a tiny voice from near their toes. It was a snail.

"You should do what I do," said the snail. "I'm going straight inside."

"Can we come with you?" asked the little rabbits.

"No," said the snail. "There is only room for me." He popped inside his shell and was gone.

Then the little rabbits all ran home. They ran and ran, through the dark and the rain, until they were all back safe inside their burrow.

And there was their kind, soft mama waiting for them.

"Sorry, sorry, sorry!" cried the three little rabbits. "Please, can we help you with the work?"

But their mama said, "My dears, you are growing and growing. There will be plenty of work for you to do. But now you must wash your ears and nibble up your supper."

The hungry, sleepy little rabbits washed their ears. They nibbled up their supper. Then they each crawled into their sleeping corners.

And guess what? Someone had made each one just a little bit bigger.

Now who do you think had done that?

Jungle, Jungle!

Jungle, jungle! Sounds of the jungle!
"Squawk! Squawk!" Who is that?

A rainbow-striped bird with shiny feathers covering her back, and long sleek tail feathers stretching down. Her beak is hooked, top and bottom, and her eye is beady.

"Squawk! Squawk! I'm a macaw," says Macaw proudly.

Jungle, jungle! Sounds of the jungle.
"Croak! Croak!" Who is that?

A slippy, slimy amphibian with leathery skin, and large staring eyes that move around. Her toes are terribly sticky and help her climb.

"Croak! Croak! I'm a tree frog," croaks Tree Frog proudly.

Jungle, jungle! Sounds of the jungle.
"O-o! O-o!" Who is that?

A big, wide-eyed mammal with long, orangey hair. She likes chewing leaves and fruit, and spends most of her life swinging through the trees.

"O-o! O-o! I'm an orangutan," says Orangutan proudly.

Jungle, jungle! Sounds of the jungle.
"Hi-ss! Hi-sssss!" Who is that?

A long-bodied reptile with scaly skin, who twists and turns on the forest floor, slithering and sliding. His eyes are keen, and he flicks out his forked tongue.

"Hi-ss! Hi-sssss! I'm a swamp-snake," hisses Swamp-snake proudly.

Jungle, jungle! Sounds of the jungle.
"Squelch! Squelch!" Who is that?

A dangerous mammal with not much hair. A creeping, frightening beast. Squelch! Squelch! Who can it be?

"Hide! Hide! Everyone hide," calls Snake.

"Wait!" calls Orangutan. "Who can it be? Let's wait and see."

"Wait to be snapped by the jaws of a croc?" squawks Macaw.

"Wait to be torn by a leopard's sharp teeth?" croaks Tree Frog.

"Wait, wait!" replies Orangutan. "I really want to know who it is—don't you?"

So they wait and see a two-legged, two-armed mammal, standing up and dressed in green. His two bright eyes are beady, aware. They are looking all around him, looking for someone, but who can it be?

"O-o, OK," whispers Orangutan. "Let's hide everyone—O-o! NOW!"

Macaw hides high in the canopy of leaves. Tree Frog hides low on a waxy leaf. Snake curls his body by the swamp.

And Orangutan swings away, up, up into the tree, as fast as her strong arms can carry her.

Squelch! Hunter's footsteps. Squelch! Very near!

"Big breath, everyone. All together now!"

"Help me! Help!" calls the frightened hunter.

Orangutan sees the hunter running, and calls out

loudly to her friends: "Big breath . . . everyone . . . all together, now!"

"Squawk! O-o! Croak! Hiss! Squawk! O-o! Croak! Hiss!" scream all the animals.

The squelching footsteps go squelch, squelch, squelch ever so quickly the opposite way. And after the silence come the other sounds, the sounds of the jungle.

Jungle, jungle! Sounds of the jungle.
Squawk! O-o! Croak! Hi-ss! Ha! Ha! Ha!

Roly and Poly

Roly and Poly are polar bears. They live in the cold, frozen north, where the wind blows and the snow snows. Roly and Poly like to play in the ice and the snow. They run and throw snowballs. They slide and skate. They play chasing games all day. They roll down the snowy slopes. They laugh and tumble. They ride on the icebergs. They swim in the navy-blue sea. They are very,

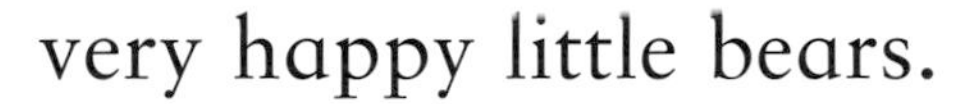

very happy little bears.

"Listen to me!" cries Roly, playing a tune by hitting a row of icicles with a stick.

"Now listen to me!" cries Poly, shouting "Hello! Hello!" in a loud voice into an echoing cave. The echoing cave shouts "Hello!" back at him.

"Listen to us!" shout Roly and Poly together, as their voices boom out a really loud, Big Bear song. They stamp out a merry dance together—moving round and round in circles over the snow.

"This is fun!" laughs Roly.

"This is great!" laughs Poly.

"Watch me!" shouts Roly, jumping to catch the biggest snowflakes you have ever seen.

"Watch me!" shouts Poly, leaping across a gap in the ice.

"Watch us!" shout Roly and Poly together, laughing as they slide all the way down from the Icy Ridge to the Deep Green Pool.

Splash! Splash! The two little bears tumble into the

freezing water.

"This is fun!" laughs Roly.

"This is great!" laughs Poly.

The bears' fur coats are soft and deep and cozy. They can stay warm all day, no matter how much the wind blows and the snow snows.

The air fills with their steamy breath as the bears climb out of the water and run down to the sea.

"I am tired now!" says Roly.

"So am I," says Poly.

"Let's sit down for a rest!" says Roly.

"What a good idea," says Poly.

The two bears look around them.

"That big gray rock looks like a good place to sit!" says Roly, pointing to a shape sticking out of the sea.

"Ooh, yes," says Poly. "It is nice and smooth."

Roly and Poly jump onto the big, smooth, gray rock and settle down for a rest before they begin playing their games again.

"This is a good rock!" says Poly.

"It's a great rock!" laughs Roly.

"I don't remember seeing it here before!" says Poly.

"No!" says Roly, "It must be a new one."

"I really am feeling very sleepy now!" says Roly.

"So am I," says Poly.

The two bears yawn and stretch, and then sit back to back. They lean against each other. They watch the lapping waves below.

First Roly's eyes start to close. Then Poly's eyes slide shut. In

no time at all both bears are fast asleep.

The sky grows dark. The stars begin to twinkle. The moon rises, big and silvery.

All of a sudden, the gray rock starts to move. It slips out into the cold sea. It moves past the icebergs and through the waves. It bobs along, following the path of the moon.

In fact, the gray rock is not a gray rock at all.

It is a humpback whale. She has just woken up and decided to go for a swim. She has no idea that two little bears are fast asleep on her back. The whale decides to dive down. The icy-cold water rushes up around her.

"Yeow!" yells Roly, waking up in the water.

"Yeow!" yells Poly, as waves splash onto his face.

The two bears are floating in the dark water—and they're a long way from home.

"Yeow!" they both call out together. "Yeow!"

Whale hears the bears' loud cries and comes back up to the surface.

"What are you two little bears doing out here at night?" she asks.

"I don't know!" says Roly.

"I don't know!" says Poly.

"We don't know!" say Roly and Poly together, and they start to cry.

"Well, I'd better take you home," says Whale. The two bears climb up onto her back.

"Your back looks a lot like the gray rock that we sat on," says Roly.

"I think your back *is* the gray rock that we sat on," says Poly.

Once they realize that they will soon be safe at home, Roly and Poly enjoy their moonlight ride.

"This is fun!" laughs Roly.
"This is great!" laughs Poly.

"Thank you!" say Roly and Poly together.

Before long they are home again. Mother Bear is delighted to see that her little bears are safe. She gives Whale a real polar bear hug. Whale swims off, waving goodbye with her huge tail.

"Goodbye!" says Roly.

"Goodbye!" says Poly.

Tumbling

In jumping and tumbling
We spend the whole day,
Till night by arriving
Has finished our play.

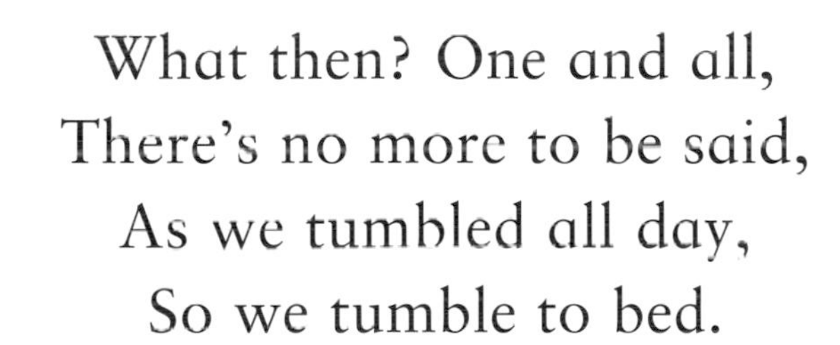

What then? One and all,
There's no more to be said,
As we tumbled all day,
So we tumble to bed.

Brahms's Lullaby

Lullaby, and good night,
With roses bedight,
With lilies overspread,
Is my baby's sweet bed.

Lay you down now, and rest,
May your slumber be blessed!
Lay you down now, and rest,
May thy slumber be blessed!

Lullaby, and good night,
You're your mother's delight;
Shining angels beside
My darling abide.

Soft and warm is your bed,
Close your eyes and rest your head.
Soft and warm is your bed,
Close your eyes and rest your head.

Johannes Brahms

We Won't Budge!

It was a hot, hot day in a hot, hot country. The watering holes were definitely the coolest place to be. But there had been no rain for days, so there was just enough water for one group of animals at a time to stand in the watering hole. The animals decided to take turns. Today it was the turn of the hippos, and one thing was for sure . . . the hippos were definitely not going to budge.

"We're cool," they gloated noisily to the other animals.

"Pleeeeease!" whined the sweating vultures near the edge of the water. "Could we pleeeeease have a teensy-weensy turn?"

But the hippos just chanted: "We won't budge!" So the vultures tap-tap-tapped on the hippos' hard skin with their sharp beaks to teach them a lesson. But hippos are thick-skinned in more ways than one, and they didn't feel a thing.

"Pleasssssssse!" hissed the snakes, slithering near the edge of the water. "Could we pleasssssssse have a slithery slice of a turn?"

But the hippos just chanted: "We won't budge!"

"We won't budge!"

So the snakes coiled their long bodies tightly around the hippos' legs and tried to pull them out! But hippos are strong in more ways than one, and they won't ever move unless they want to.

"Plehee-hee-ease!" neighed the zebras, hoping for a tiny share of the water. "Could we plehee-hee-ease have the thinnest stripe of a turn?"

But the hippos just chanted: "We won't budge!" So the zebras all pawed at the ground with their hooves, trying to scare the hippos away. But hippos are brave in more ways than one, and they didn't even blink an eyelid. And one thing was for sure . . . and they said it again: "WE WON'T BUDGE!"

As the sun grew hotter, more and more animals came to the watering hole. They stood around its edge, staring across at the selfish hippos. But the hippos weren't going to budge even for the gentle antelopes, who helped them out by swatting flies from their ears with their swishing tails. Today, those cool hippos standing in the cool water of the watering hole were not going to budge—for anyone!

Suddenly there came a noise that made the hippos look up. Every ear of every hippo twitched, and listened. It was a noise that made the antelopes and zebras and snakes and vultures sprint and gallop and slither and fly away in an instant.

DER-UM! DER-UM! DR-UM! DR-UM!
DRM! DRM! DRM!

The hippos stood up. Their eyes grew wider and their big, strong legs trembled. Their hard skins shivered, and they didn't know what to do.

"Help!" whispered the littlest hippo very quietly.

"We won't budge," whispered the biggest hippo even more quietly.

There was silence, except for the thundering dust cloud approaching the watering hole.

"WE WILL BUDGE!" exclaimed all the hippos together, as they rushed away.

The thundering dust was actually an enomous herd of heavy elephants. They were thirsty and hot, and they weren't going to be stopped from cooling their feet. So the elephants kept running toward the watering hole until they splashed right into the middle of the pool.

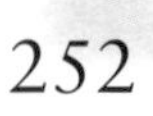

"Aaaaah!" sighed the elephants, trumpeting their happiness. And all the other animals (except those brave old hippos) sneaked back to take a look at them.

"One thing is definitely for sure," called the sweating vultures. "Those cool elephants are not going to budge for anyone."

But it didn't matter, because the elephants saw how hot and bothered the vultures and the snakes and the antelopes were under the scorching sun. They counted: "One and . . . two and . . . three and . . .". Then they sucked up the water into their long, rubbery trunks, pointed, squinted, aimed, and fired the water at the animals all around.

"Aaaah!"

"Aaaah!" sighed the antelopes.
"Aaaah!" neighed the zebras.
"Aaaah!" hissed the snakes.

"Aaaaaaah!" sighed the hippos, who were standing a long way off, watching everything. If only they could be sprayed too. And slowly, very slowly, hardly knowing what they were doing, the hot hippos made their way back to the watering hole.

But there was only room for one group of animals at a time to stand in the water. Now it was the elephants' turn. And one thing was for sure. "WE WON'T BUDGE!" they called out, when they saw the hippos approaching.

"Pleeeeeeeeeease!" pleaded the hippos. "Could we plehee-hee-ease have the chunkiest chunk of a turn?"

"No you can't!" trumped the cool elephants. "That's just greedy."

"Hurrah!" cheered the antelopes, the snakes, the zebras, and the vultures. They all remembered very well that the hippos hadn't budged for them—or squirted them.

So the hot hippos, with their burning-hot skins, tramped away from the watering hole. And the elephants watched them go, and felt very sorry for them. They counted: "One and . . . two and . . . three and . . ." Then they sucked up the water into their long trunks, pointed, squinted, aimed, and fired at the hippos.

"Aaaaaaaaaaaaaaaaah!" sighed the hippos.

And one thing was for sure . . . they were definitely NOT going to budge.

The Man in the Moon

The man in the moon looked out of the moon,
Looked out of the moon and said,
"'Tis time for all children on the earth
To think about getting to bed!"